Chickens Come Home to Roost

Published

By

Edson Mazira

ISBN 978-0-7974-8364-4

Chickens Come Home to Roost

© Edson Mazira, 2020

ACKNOWLEDGEMENTS

I reserve this moment to thank my relatives and my friends for their contributions to the development of this project.
Be blessed.

CONTENTS

CHAPTER

1

SHERRY Banda halted and cried, "Help!" She trembled in the middle of the Eden Forest. The thorns of the jungle had shredded her clothes and pricked her shins. The sweat flowing from her disheveled hair had soaked her body. Her eyes were red and wet with tears. Mucus streamed under her nose, and it bathed her lips.

She gaped as she took a look of everything around her. The awful caves and the fierce holes made her mind create horrible illusions, which caused her heart to pound heavily. Twirling with her shaking hands on her head, she found almost everything in the jungle unfamiliar.

She floundered through the grass and skirted the bushes, hoping to meet Bob and his friends.

"Are the boys still waiting for me near the road?" She shook her head from side to side.

For sure, the boys had lost their patience and gone home.

Stumbled by a tree stub, she fell and lay flat on a carpet of decayed and fresh leaves.

Some hours later, a gecko crawled over her forehead and roused her. She was astonished to see that the sun had already been swallowed by the western horizon. It was now midnight.

Time flies. She glanced at her wrist, as if she was wearing a watch, and then looked up. *Thanks for the bright moon.*

The breeze of the night swept over her body and slightly shook small tree branches such that some of their leaves—which were not intact—fell off one by one. She sat down and huddled for warmth.

The night itself was almost silent; nothing—except the hooting owls, the yelping jackals and the laughing hyenas, all in the distance—could be heard making sounds.

"I can't stay here," she whispered, got up and sneaked out of the place. She went all her way turning her head to watch both sides and behind her back. As she walked, the dew from the grass soaked her wounded shins, and she felt some pain and realised that she had been injured on the biggest toe of her right leg and that she had lost her shoes.

"Where're my shoes?" She looked around.

Ignoring the shoes, she began to think about her baby son, and her eyes welled up with tears.

Suddenly, an alarming scream and a rattling sound of falling stones echoed in the Dead Gorge, a huge gorge in the Eden Forest, whose name came after many carcasses and corpses were being found dumped in it.

Hours later, after the noise, a big red snake with several black spots crossed over Sherry's stomach as she lay unconscious on the floor of the Dead Gorge, her back in the mud. Its coldness roused her into consciousness—she sat up, frightened, and looked around in confusion, coughing from choke, but did not see it. She tried to recall what had happened to her. There was a cluster of stones around her. Her legs and her hands had fresh bruises. She lifted up her face to the gorge bank next to her and shook her head.

"So I fell down from there?" she said, tears in her eyes.

For a while, she remained seated at the same position, musing. She turned her pale face over her right shoulder and rested her chin on it watching her back. She searched all around to see if she could find her way out. The area was unfamiliar. There were no known directions to take. Finally, she struggled up and limped down the gorge, staggering.

"Ah!" Before she had gone far, she arced her eyebrows and stopped, her palms covering her open mouth. She had caught sight of a big snake lying across the path she was following. It was the one that had harmlessly wriggled over her, which she had not seen.

Sherry backed off, panting. Her eyes remained focused on the snake and monitored its movement. She retraced through the place where she had been lying unconscious and did not turn back until her right heel hit a body, which she quickly felt was of a mammal. Suddenly, a buzz from disturbed insects forced her to look back. They were greenflies feasting on a corpse. Without daring to find out who the dead person was, she sprinted away, screaming.

*

About a kilometre to the west, in the same jungle, Daniel Sango—a young man in his early thirties—was staring at a cave in a baobab tree. Some areas of the Eden Forest were familiar to him. He had once visited them with his late father, Walter Sango, but that was a very long way back when he was only ten years old. Fortunately, the videos and the pictures his father had taken before he kicked the bucket always reminded him of the places.

What cave is that? He frowned and narrowed his eyes. He looked all around, and his heart throbbed. Little perspiration formed on his forehead.

Immediately, a new thought visited him: *Maybe what I'm looking for is inside it.* He smiled without parting his lips, wiped off the perspiration and advanced to it. The cave was calm and warm. He smiled again, sat down and slightly patted on the floor. *Yes, this is it.* As if he was on his bed in his house, he lay down and rolled to the other side. *This place is clean. Who owns it?*

Suddenly, 'somebody' who owned the cave wriggled in, his scales shining brightly. The snake looked exactly the same with the one he had been encountering in his nightmares. Daniel got up and grappled the wall with his back. His heart was palpitating fast, and his body began to perspire abnormally. His eyes searched around for another possible point of exit, but there was none. The snake coiled up at the centre, hissing.

*

At the Dead Gorge, Sherry felt somewhat re-lieved. She had managed to climb out of the gorge. She now wandered west for about a kilometre. There, she heard a deafening sound of something charging from her right side. Wondering what it was, she felt her jaws quiver-ing and her knees weakening. She knelt down and placed her face into her cupped hands. No sooner had she done so than Daniel knocked her down and fell nearby.

The two just blinked at each other, with open mouths, but no words were uttered. They stayed like that for a moment, making sure that the distance between them was not reduced.

A few minutes later, Daniel pulled up a brave man's face and broke the silence: "Who're you?"

"My name... I'm Sherry. You?"

"Daniel. Daniel Sango. And your surname?"

"Banda."

Sherry always narrowed her eyes and looked straight into Daniel's as he spoke. Daniel also did the same. The distance between them re-mained unchanged.

"Is anyone after you?" she asked curiously.

He shook his head: "No." *Why asking this?*

"No? But you came here sprinting."

"I..."

"Yes."

"...saw a dangerous snake in a cave." He narrated the whole story to her including the reason he had reached the Eden Forest and how his late father had been haunting him in his dreams.

Sherry blinked out some tears when she heard about the death of Daniel's father, who was found dead in the jungle about 16 years ago. That reminded her to tell Daniel about the dead man in the gorge.

"What brought you here?" He looked at her up and down. "What happened to you? You're wounded."

She pulled a face and lowered her voice: "My story's too long." She began to sob.

"Just try to tell me."

She rubbed off her tears. "I was kidnapped by four men. They wanted to kill me.

"The whole night, I slept here. I don't know how to get out of this place."

Daniel shook his head gently and crawled close to her. "I can help you. I know the way out. We have to go straight to the police." He stood up. "Get up. We've to go before it gets hot."

She got up slowly, paying attention to her bruises.

"May I carry you?" He stretched out his hands.

"No. I can do it myself."

The two trudged through the thickets and passed by the place where Sherry had seen the dead body, but they did not get close to identify it.

After trekking for some time, Sherry began to gasp and pull her legs. She felt her bruises itching. They stopped and found a place to rest.

"Do you really know where we're going?"

Daniel remained silent. After a few minutes, he said, "Let's go."

"I'm still tired."

"We'll find another place to rest soon."

"Help me get up."

He held her hand carefully and pulled her up.

As they walked away, minute insects buzzed around their heads. Some of them got stuck as they landed on sweat.

"Look!" Daniel pointed at the road excitedly. "There, it is! The road!"

A brilliant smile tore Sherry's dry lips. She sighed and leaped around, singing.

Now, they waited for the vehicles to carry them, but there was no sign of any. The road was quiet—no sound, no what. The only sounds were of the rustling leaves being blown by slight winds and of one or two owls hooting from afar, which made Sherry stick close to Daniel.

Sometime later, soon after the sun had set, a vehicle arrived and stopped for them. It was a yellow taxi with only two red letters G.J. inscribed on its white number plates.

Inside it, there was the driver alone, a slim lady clad in a white suit, a white t-shirt and a pair of white shoes. She had long black hair, whose ends touched her shoulders. Her eyes blinked under artificial eyelashes and penciled eyebrows. Her mouth wore some dark lipstick. Golden earrings swung under her ears. In all, the makeup made her round face look more gorgeous. As her hands held the steering, a golden watch sparkled round her left wrist. Also sparkling, but round her neck, were two—if not three—loose necklaces made of gold too.

Sherry and Daniel greeted her and occupied the back seat.

After driving for about a kilometre without talking, the driver broke the silence: "You're such lucky people to get my car. These days, very, very few drivers use this road. Many of them fear the ghost of Gertrude Jena, a woman murdered here 16 years ago. Fortunately, her baby girl was saved."

"What a sad story!" Sherry said.

"Very sad, Sherry," she said.

Sherry gaped and looked in the view mirror reflecting the driver's face to see if she could recognise her, but that was a stranger. "How did you know my name?"

"I know you, Sherry Banda, and your father, Jacob Banda."

"From where?"

"Long story." She pulled a face, and her eyes welled up with tears, which she rubbed off with a piece of cloth.

"You look like sisters," Daniel commented, looking at them one by one.

Sherry shrugged and shouted, "Don't be stupid, Dan! Are you out of your mind?"

"I'm sorry."

"Anyway"—the driver chipped in—"how's your father?"

Sherry paused for a moment and then replied, "For now, I can't say he's okay because I don't know his whereabouts. He's missing."

"Really?" Her voice was low, and she blinked out some tears. "I'm so sorry. That's a piece of disturbing news. Did anyone report it to the police?"

"Yes." She was nodding. "My mother did."

"Did you say, '...my mother...'?" Surprised, she looked her in the eyes.

"Yeah!" She nodded again, a bit confused, and began to think about the driver's question: *"Did you say, '...my mother...'?"*

CHAPTER

2

A T around 7 p.m., Sherry and Daniel were in the charge office of Magamba Central Police Station. She stood facing Constable Ncube on a tall stool behind a wooden counter; he was filling in a form for her.

"You see this form?" He looked her straight in the eyes, handing her the form.

"Yeah."

"You take it to the hospital. The nurses have to treat you first."

She nodded.

Daniel frowned. "What about her report? Isn't it important?"

The constable leered at him first and then said, "Cool down, Mister. I know what I'm doing. Can't you see this tape recorder?"

"I'm sorry if I have offended you."

"It's okay, Mister." He looked at Sherry. "Come back right here after the hospital."

"Thank you." She walked away, limping.

A police ambulance was already outside the charge office, waiting for her. Daniel stayed behind so that he could help the police locate the corpse in the Dead Gorge.

The police officers chose a helicopter to attend the crime scene because there were no roads to take them straight into the Eden Forest.

Among them, there was Detective Sergeant Green Ash, a committed detective.

At that time, Detective Chief Inspector Nyoka, DS Green's superior, was the officer in charge of the CID Homicide Section. He was as influential as his retired predecessor Detective Chief Inspector Jacob Banda. The two were close friends.

The helicopter departed for the scene. When they reached the Eden Forest, they searched for the gorge first, using the lights of the helicopter. Two officers had binoculars. Daniel opened his eyes wide enough not to miss it; he hardly blinked.

At last, after the search that had nearly fractured their necks, they found the gorge. The pilot lowered the helicopter, and they began to search for the dead body.

"You lied to us!" the pilot shouted at Daniel.

Daniel rolled his lips into his mouth, and his eyelids became a bit heavy. Shame blurred his eyes. He drooped his head.

Detective Sergeant Green leered at the pilot. "Take it easy, man. The gorge is too long and too big. Let's try that side."

"But he directed us here, didn't he?" the pilot grumbled.

"Of course, but we've not yet searched everywhere! Besides, that's not how we handle our clients, dude!" the sergeant's voice rose.

Sometime later, they spotted the corpse. The helicopter landed on a dry clearing in the gorge; it was positioned a reasonable distance from the crime scene so that it could not interfere with any evidence around the place. The detectives disembarked and walked in a single file towards the dead body, clutching their torches, guns and toolboxes. Daniel followed behind them, carrying nothing.

When they got to it, DS Green assessed the scene and suggested they work on it the following day—in daylight. In regard to that, they did not alter anything at the place.

Daniel gaped. "Why do you want to do it tomorrow?"

"We want to take a few photos of the corpse and other points of police interest first before we alter anything, so the process cannot be done at night."

"Okay."

They went back to the helicopter in the same manner they had approached the corpse, but Daniel was now in front of them, swinging his hands like a marching soldier. The whole night, they took turns to guard the scene.

*

Some minutes past the midnight hour, Detective Chief Inspector Nyoka received a phone call from Eunice Banda, Sherry's mother, informing him about Sherry.

"What do you say, Eunice?" His voice echoed. "Say it again!"

"I... I mean Sherry's missing."

"I don't tolerate that nonsense! Is that some kind of joke? Anyway, tell Bob and his friends that they owe me an explanation if she's gone for good!" He switched off the cellphone and wrestled to calm down his nerves.

Bob was Sherry's brother. He had two best friends, Matthew and Stanford. The three had a unique friendship in which they always shared their life secrets.

*

In the morning, when the sun had shown up, the detectives approached the scene and worked on it. They photographed the corpse from different angles and then moved around, carefully looking for other things of police interest. DS Green found a black wallet dropped some metres away from the corpse.

After they had photographed their points, they rolled the dead body over and were dumbfounded to see that it was Jacob Banda, Sherry's father.

Detective Sergeant Green phoned Detective Chief Inspector Nyoka and informed him about the incident.

"I'm touched, my man," DCI Nyoka sobbed. "Right now, I'm at his home. His daughter, Sherry, went missing the day before yesterday. Why this family?"

"Sherry's admitted at Magamba General Hospital. She got wounded when she was running away from some bloody kidnappers.

"She's the one who told us about the dead body."

"What did she say about it?" He placed his left hand onto his pounding chest, while the right one trembled with the cellphone on his right ear.

"She just said she saw a dead person, but she doesn't know it's her father."

"Okay, well, well, well, it's fine." He cleared his throat. "Act upon that kidnapping case, right? We've to apprehend the kidnappers and make them pay for their evil deeds."

"Thank you, sir."

"Mm, what're you planning to do with the body?"

"We're now taking it to the mortuary."

"It's okay. I'll join you there."

"Thank you, sir." After the conversation, DS Green mused for a moment and then walked back to join his team.

A few minutes later, the helicopter took off from the Eden Forest.

CHAPTER

3

AT Magamba General Hospital, in a female surgical ward, Sherry lay with her back on a high-legged bed. Her wounds were healing up. She might need another day to recover completely. Beside her sat two female police officers, Constable Mbeva and Detective Constable Tilda. They had come to record some statements from her.

"Well." Constable Mbeva, while seated, dragged her stool close to Sherry. "Can you narrate again the ordeals you faced in the Eden Forest? Take your time; don't panic."

Sherry swallowed her saliva and remained silent for a while. *She thinks I'm lying,* she thought, *and she wants to trap me. The—*

"Please," Detective Constable Tilda complained, a made-up frown on her forehead, "don't waste our time."

"But your friend has—"

"She hasn't told you to waste our time, has she?"

"I'm sorry. It's like, mm, I... At around 2 p.m., I hired a taxi from Magamba town, intending to go home. To my surprise, the taxi diverted the route and drove to a different destination. I—"

DC Tilda sneered. "What day was it? Type of the taxi?"

"Like what I said at first, because of the powder, I lost almost my entire memory; I can't remember what day it was. But the taxi's silver; that's all I can say about it because I'm not familiar with car types." She paused for her comment.

"Okay." DC Tilda folded her arms onto her breasts. "Go ahead."

"Thank you. I tried to shout for help, but the two men at the back seat grabbed me and tied my mouth with the towel that had the powder, which caused me to drowse and lose my senses.

"The last place I found myself in was the jungle. Thank God, I managed to escape from the kidnappers.

"That's all I can say about it."

Constable Mbeva pulled a face and said, "It's okay, Sherry. Everything's *gonna* be fine, but you've forgotten to describe the kidnappers."

She looked at her and said in a low voice, "I described them in the first—"

"Yes, we know that"—DC Tilda chipped in—"but describe them again. Isn't everything you said in the second narration a repeat?"

"It is," Sherry agreed.

"So," Detective Tilda said, a smirk on her face, "don't mind it; just repeat the descriptions of the kidnappers as well."

Constable Mbeva nodded: "Yes."

"The men were four." She paused for some seconds. "The driver had dreadlocks and was light in complexion. The one next to the driver was dark and had a balding head. The other two with me at the back seat were dark too. All of them had medium bodies. This is all I still remember about them."

"Thank you, Sherry," DC Tilda said. "We're doing all this to help you; we promise to apprehend the criminals." She stood up, yawning, and stretched herself.

"Here you are." Constable Mbeva handed her a written statement. "Read and sign right here if you agree with its contents. Just after your signature, write down registration numbers of your national ID card. Thank you."

Sherry took the statement and carefully went through it. Immediately, Detective Chief Inspector Nyoka and Eunice, Sherry's mother, entered the ward. Sherry had just finished reading and was about to sign it when DCI Nyoka saw it all and shouted from the door: "Wait! Give it to me first!"

The shout took everybody in the ward aback. The junior police officers came to attention and saluted him first, but he did not respond. He just leered at them. Sherry sheepishly handed him the statement. He read it. "Now you can sign it." He handed it back, nodding. "It's good and true."

"It's good and true." DC Tilda scratched her head, thoughtful. *What does he know about it?*

Eunice inclined her head to the left, looking Sherry in the eyes. "How're you, my daughter? You're the only one I have."

"Don't worry, Mom." She smiled, signing the statement. "I'm recovering. Sister Claris is taking good care of me; she's a kind nurse."

Eunice looked at Claris, a grin on her face. "Thank you, Sister Claris."

"You're welcome." A thin smile spread from Claris' small oily lips to her ears.

"So, Sister Claris, when'll she be discharged?"

"Hmm, the doctor attending her said tomorrow."

"Okay. That's good," she said and then thought: *I can't tell her about the death of her father right now. I'll do it tomorrow when she's discharged.*

Constable Mbeva and Detective Constable Tilda left the ward.

At that moment, DS Green Ash and his team of detectives were at Magamba Mortuary, which was in the same premise with the hospital. They were handing over the dead body to the mortuary attendants.

DS Green received a phone call from DCI Nyoka. "Hello, sir," he answered expectantly.

"Where're you now?"

"Magamba Mortuary."

"Wait for me; I'm coming there." He ended the conversation promptly.

Eunice looked at him suspiciously. "Where to?"

"Nowhere. I'm around. Just want to meet Green outside. I'll be back soon." He was putting his cellphone back into its pouch. He strutted out and left almost everybody nonplussed.

At the mortuary, the sergeant told him about the scene: "Among the objects we found around the scene, there's a black wallet with Bob's national ID card and other documents."

"Which Bob?" He was astounded.

"Bob Banda, the deceased's own son."

"Ah! This is weird! Did you write it down?" He folded his arms onto his chest. Little sweat could be seen emerging on his forehead.

He nodded: "Of course, sir. It's of police interest."

DCI Nyoka tottered backwards and sat down on the ground.

"Are you fine, sir?" He strode towards and reached out to help him.

"Back off! I don't need your help! Give me the wallet right now! Don't trouble a family already in trouble! It's mourning for its breadwinner, and you want to count its son as a suspect on top of that! Isn't this adding salt to the injury?"

"Sir, I'm sorry for causing you so much disappointment, but I'm not going to give it to you without proper handover and takeover. Thank you, sir." He strode back.

"Are you teaching me police work? Are you challenging my rank?" He stood up, foaming at the mouth, and glanced at him. "You're refusing to obey lawful instructions from your superior! This is insubordination!" He pointed his shaking finger at him. "Be very careful!"

DS Green shook his head. "I only refuse the procedure with which you want me to hand the wallet over to you; it's not lawful at all."

The officer in charge strutted back to the ward, boiling with anger. He took Eunice and drove her home. After dropping her off, he drove back to his office. There, he walked slowly right round his office desk, his hands folded on his chest. Some tears were on his cheeks.

There was a short knock on the door, and he quickly rubbed off the tears. Detective Superintendent Edwards, his superior, opened the door and got in.

"Nyoka, I'm here to pass my condolences for the death of your best friend."

"Thank you, sir."

*

The following day, at around 9 a.m., Sherry was discharged from the hospital. As she approached her home, she reduced her paces and gaped at a fleet of cars haphazardly parked outside the yard. She walked in, doubting if she had really been discharged. She pinched herself to check if she was awake, and the pain knocked her real senses.

Eunice peered through the window and saw her confused daughter shambling towards the house. She rushed out and embraced her.

Sherry suspected that something bad had happened to her missing father. "Where's Daddy, Mama?"

Her mother said nothing; she just wept, tears and mucus flowing down her face.

"Tell me, please!" She was crying. "Where's my father? Bob, come and tell me! Where's Daddy?"

Some of the mourners came and took her aside. They told her the story and gave her some counseling. It touched her after she had learnt that the dead body which she had encountered in the Dead Gorge was of her father.

That same day was the day for a postmortem. Eunice was invited to witness it. DCI Nyoka and DS Green were present during the postmortem process.

After about three hours, the postmortem results came out. They were made confidential. At the moment, they were only for the police to proceed with their investigations.

The burial was conducted on the following day. Jacob Banda received a great honour from the police because he was an ex-police officer, who had served in the police force for more than twenty years. He had just retired a few months before his death.

*

One cool day, Detective Sergeant Green sat in his house, reading a piece of newspaper with Jacob Banda's story:

EDMAZ NEWS

THURSDAY   20 JANUARY 2016

EX-DETECTIVE CHIEF INSPECTOR JACOB BANDA FOUND DEAD

It happened by sheer coincidence. The ex-officer in charge of the CID Homicide Section of Magamba Central Police, Detective Chief Inspector Jacob Banda (50), was found dead in the Eden Forest by his own daughter, Sherry Banda (18). It's allegedly reported that, on the 7th day of September in 2016, Jacob Banda did not return home after he had taken a general stroll.

Eunice Banda (45), the deceased's wife, confirmed his missing and reported the matter to Magamba Central Police Station.

Chief Inspector Mupota, the provincial police spokesperson, confirmed that the former police officer was found dead in the Eden Forest by his daughter.

The chief inspector said, "It's reported that the girl had been kidnapped into the jungle. This makes us suspect that those kidnappers have something to do with the death of Jacob Banda.

"It's my pleasure to let people know that there are other similar cases that occurred in the Eden Forest before this one. In 1998, there was a lady called Gertrude Jena; she was found dead in the Eden Forest. Thank God, the woman's daughter was saved.

"Postmortem results confirmed that she had died of food poison.

"At the same time, the police also found a dead body of a man stabbed with a knife; his name was Walter Sango.

"Today, we're talking of Jacob Banda, who also died of food poison. It's so shocking that this food-poison killing started about 16 years ago, and we don't know when and where it'll end. This is really horrible.

"However, as the police, we're still working on the crimes indefatigably. One day, we'll bring the perpetrators to the face of the law. Thank you."

****

By Senior Reporter Mvurayatota

"What happened exactly in 1998?" He was stroking his chin. "Did Walter Sango poison Gertrude Jena and then committed suicide? If no, why then was his body found next to hers?

"Gertrude's baby was near the dead bodies; why was she not killed?" He shrugged and stood up. He walked to his bedroom and looked at himself in a big mirror. A short man with dark complexion he was. His hair was always kept short, and he loved to keep a small moustache.

Sometime later, he went back to the sitting room and looked at the newspaper again, scratching his head.

"Jacob Banda," he said, tears forming in his eyes, "saved my poor father when those ruthless muggers attacked him on his way home from the market. I promised Daddy I would join the police to deal with the criminals. Yes, now I'm a policeman, what am I doing with it?"

For sure, Green's father would have been murdered one evening had Officer Jacob Banda not reacted fast and rescued him. Four street robbers, having been disturbed, ran away and left him with six knife cuts, which took time to heal up.

*

About two kilometres to the west of DS Green's residence lay a low density suburb called Golden. There lived a business mogul whose name was Clifford Kauri. He lived in a protected mansion and had many bodyguards. Wherever he travelled, a convoy of latest cars always escorted him. The guy was a friend of many police bosses, and he used to assist the police with many resources. Many times, he visited the offices of the CID Homicide Section mainly to see DCI Nyoka. That was a certain type of influential people in the community.

The other type was of Bomber and his friends. They lived in a ghetto, where they were widely known for indulging themselves with drugs. Their gang was comprised of Queen, Diesel, Razor, Planet and Bomber himself as their leader. Those names were just street names; their real ones were not well known.

Bomber and Diesel always kept dreadlocks on their heads. Razor and Planet liked their clean-shaven heads. Queen was for wigs, and she could change them frequently. Her body was a lure. Her complexion was light, and that was her natural skin. She was a popular hooker. Erstwhile, she was Clifford's side chick.

*

DS Green folded his newspaper and put it aside. He stood up and attended to a knock on the door.

"Wow! Come in! You're welcome!" he said excitedly.

"Thank you so much, Green." Detective Constable Tilda got in.

"It's a blessing to have you in my quarters."

"Really?"

"Sure." He led her to the sofas, where he had been sitting since morning. "Make yourself comfortable; the place is all yours. Just sit anywhere."

"Haha, my friend," she said, laughing, "can I sit on this glass table of yours? This is the meaning of anywhere. Haha!

"Anyway, let me sit here." She sat in the sofa opposite to the one in which he had sat.

"How's work?"

She clicked her tongue and slouched back in the sofa: "It's boring. I wish I were on time off like you."

"Really?" He was caressing his chin.

"Am here to let you know there'll be a section meeting tomorrow. It's for all the members including those on time off."

"What time?"

"9 a.m."

"Thank you."

She licked her dry lips. "Have you cooked anything for me? I'm too hungry."

"Didn't know you're coming, sorry."

"Now, am here."

"Take over the kitchen. All the pots are clean."

"No." She laughed. "Let me die of the hunger if this is the case. I can't cook for myself; you're the one supposed to cook for the visitor."

"Haha"—he shrugged—"it's up to you."

The two chatted until they were left with no interesting stories to share, but only yawns. Finally, she left for her home, and he accompanied her.

CHAPTER

4

DETECTIVE Sergeant Green Ash woke up early in the morning of Monday and prepared for the meeting. He took himself into a long-sleeved crispy sky-blue shirt, a silver tie with dark-blue stripes, a navy-blue suit and a pair of black leather shoes. When he had put everything in order, he picked up a black briefcase and went to his car.

As usual, the venue for the meeting was going to be the CID conference room. The place was furnished with dark luxury chairs and two long well-polished tables. Its walls were creamy. The ceiling was white. The floor was a mixed pattern of black and white tiles. A 52-inch plasma television was fixed on one side of the walls.

When DS Green entered the conference room, everyone was already there, waiting for DCI Nyoka, the chairing person. No sooner had he sat down than DCI Nyoka walked in, wearing a don't-play-with-me face. They greeted him, but his words refused to come out through his thick lips.

"This room is stinking!" His voice was now loud and clear, and it was trembling. He leered at DS Green and sat down on a rocking chair placed at the end of one of the tables. "Does your own home look like this, Green? This place looks like a dumping site? Why didn't you tell your subordinates to clean it?

"You don't have leadership qualities, my friend. I'm very sorry for this truth."

They looked around and then at one another with awe. In their eyes, the room was sparkling with cleanness. Although it was so, DS Green did not attempt to argue with his superior at all; he simply apologised: "Sorry, sir!"

The meeting started. DC Tilda, the secretary, sat near the chairing person, taking down new minutes into her police diary.

"I thank you, Chaplain, for the opening prayer. I thank you, Tilda, for reading the minutes of the previous meeting. I thank you all for your presence." DCI Nyoka paused and took a swig from a glass of water. "Our main agenda is about the death of Jacob Banda, my best friend. I'm sure we all know what happened to him. He was found dead in the Eden Forest, his body already decomposing in the Dead Gorge. This is pathetic.

"Are you following me?"

"Yes, sir," they all answered in unison, some nodding.

He continued: "It's already in our files that he died after eating poisoned food. Therefore, every food or beer outlet in this town must be haunted.

"The man I'm talking about was a glutton and a drunkard. Do you get what I mean?"

"Sir!" the detectives chorused.

He coughed and continued: "Some of you really need retraining. It's clear that some of you are immature.

"One of you whom I always respected and regarded as a clever detective finally showed me his foolishness. He brought Bob's wallet and recorded it as a piece of concrete evidence linked to the death of Jacob Banda." He paused for a short time and then said, "Is this what we expect from a mature detective? Is that concrete evidence, my comrades?"

His subordinates just looked at one another; none passed a comment.

"This is not the first murder you have ever encountered. You have been working on a number of them. Haven't you ever noticed that criminals use other people's ID cards during the commission of the crimes? You must have noticed this trick.

"Bob is a complainant, not an accused person. Don't harass him and his family; you need to sympathise with them instead. Do you get me?

"Treat people with caution and observe their human rights.

"Sometimes, you definitely lose nothing by ignoring some things. Don't personalize things that are meant for all."

Some agreed with what he was saying; meanwhile, others slightly showed gestures of disagreement.

"Sir, sorry to say this. I know you're on me. You seem to have gotten me wrong. I'm not, and

I was not, saying the wallet in question is the evidence that Bob is part of this crime; I said it's one of the objects we just picked up from the scene—that's all. In this way, I don't think it'll be wise to hand it over to Bob without asking him one or two questions," Sergeant Green explained steadily. "Who knows?" he asked rhetorically and shrugged, throwing away his hands. "His answers might lead us to the criminals."

"I'm not against that idea of yours, Green. But, as you'll be questioning him, you've to bear it in mind that he's the complainant, as I said earlier, not the accused, and that he's mourning for his beloved father. Do you get me?" He stared at DS Green.

He nodded.

The meeting lasted for about an hour, but nobody got any chance to express their own ideas. The officer in charge just served them with the type of meal he liked.

"Before I call for a closing prayer to end this meeting, let me announce it to you that I'll be on vac. leave very soon if it's approved. Therefore, I urge you to treat this case with caution. I don't want to hear any bad news about any of you being charged for performing duty improperly. Forewarned is forearmed. There is no employment in this country; once you're discharged from this police force, you're doomed.

"I'm sorry to remind you always that the way you see TV police detectives solving their cases is different from the reality. Anyway, I don't want to sound as if I'm discouraging you, but a rebuke from your friend is better than a welcoming kiss from your enemy.

"Concerning the case of my late friend, I'm so committed that I won't distance myself from you; I'll be visiting my office regularly in order to assist you. Anytime you feel like you need my assistance, feel free to consult me. Thank y'all."

"It'll be boring without you, sir," DC Bere, one of the subordinates, commented worriedly. "Anyway, since you've promised to be with us on this case, I'm going to be one of those humble detectives to consult you."

DCI Nyoka praised him: "Thank you so much, Bere. You're a clever detective."

Bere, DC Tilda thought, slowly scratching her head, *is a trained police officer with immature mentality. How can he support the tyrannical superior who always threatens us? The threats of charges against police defaulters and discharges from the police force are now like our native language. We're employed, but we're not secure. This is bullshit.*

The meeting ended. DS Green and DC Francis, one of his subordinates, drove away from the police station and parked at a nature park nearby, where they tried to relax and refresh their boiling minds.

"Sierra Golf Tango," DC Francis called, turning to his sergeant.

"Yes?"

"Any comments about it?"

"About what?"

"The meeting."

"Mm, not bad; not bad."

DC Francis arced his eyebrows. "Really?" He paused for some seconds and then continued: "For me, it was awful. The way our boss defends Bob Banda discourages me a lot. He threatens us not to touch the Banda family. Why? What does it mean?

"This battle reminds me of a certain occasion: One superintendent from the CID Law and Order Section was transferred because he had shown some commitment in investigating cases that involved one of the government ministers. From that time, he was never promoted again until he retired. This discourages me."

"It's normal, Francis. If you were in his shoes, you would do the same. That family is his best friend's; therefore, let him fight for it. I see nothing wrong with his action." The sergeant was wiping some dust off the car dashboard.

"This is too much, Serge. DCI Nyoka has really quenched my zeal. I no longer have that burning thing in me for Jacob's case; neither do I still have it for any other business meant for the police. Let me just be neutral as long as my salary comes in with no deductions for idleness." He made a wry face of I don't care. "This isn't what I expected. Now, I understand that a colour you see with mountains—from afar—is not it when you come close. I can testify on behalf of everybody that they join this organisation with passion, but the internal system quenches it all. I'll soon quit this thing!" He nodded: "Yes."

"No, don't do that, mate. Don't quit your calling. Keep on maintaining law and order. Protect the lives of people and their property. God will bless you for that."

"Really?" He showed a little smile. "I sometimes think of quitting this career because of these tyrannical superiors who abuse their offices."

"Don't say that again, Francis. There is no employment with no top brass. If the boss isn't you, then it's another person. You must also know that every situation we face in life teaches us to be responsible people in the future. In most cases, the best leader is the one with the greatest experience."

"Sure? You can say that again, Serge. I really like your words of wisdom and encouragement."

"Hey, time's up, Francis. Let's drive home." He started the car.

*

Tuesday, the following day, was almost the same as Monday, except that the mist was a bit thicker. It was too difficult to see anything located about 50 metres away from you. There was traffic jam as it was on the previous day. Among the vehicles driving into town, there was a car for the Banda family; the family was going to be in town for some hours of the day.

First of all, the family drove to a food outlet that belonged to Clifford Kauri, the business mogul. Before Jacob Banda died, he used to frequent the same place for some delicacies.

Eunice Banda, Bob Banda and Sherry Banda occupied a table and ordered three portions of potato chips, a full roasted chicken and three coffees. After having the breakfast, they bought three teas, which they drank on their way to a city library located at the centre of the largest nature park in the town. The nature park and the library were close to the CID Headquarters and were the places DS Green usually visited to ease off some work pressure on him.

On that day, DCI Nyoka deployed his subordinates and instructed them to visit every food outlet and every beer outlet they knew. They were working on Jacob Banda's case.

DS Green did not visit any food outlet or beer outlet; instead, he visited the library. He wanted to ease off the pressure DCI Nyoka had been putting onto him since the day he refused to surrender Bob's wallet to him.

"Hi, Green." There was a familiar voice of a woman near him.

"Hi." He looked up from his book. "Wow! It's you? I never expected to see a person like you in this place, Mrs Banda."

"Sure?" Eunice walked a little and stood right in front of him, her long hands on her waist and an alluring smile on her face. A big V-shaped neck of her tight bodice exposed her protruding breasts. "What's up?"

He shrugged. "Nothing. How's your family, that is, Bob and Sherry?"

"Good." She pointed at them. "They're there."

He looked at them. "Wonderful. May you tell Bob to come for his wallet at my office? It contains his national ID card and some documents."

"Oh boy, how did you find it?" She cast her cunning eyes at her son and then back to the police detective.

"No biggie, Good Samaritan just picked it up from the streets and brought it to the police."

"Well"—she smiled—"thanks a lot. I'll tell him. When should he come?"

"Let's say tomorrow morning."

"Okay, he'll definitely do so."

"Much appreciated."

"You're welcome.

"At the moment, we're leaving the library for lunch at Kauri's Hotel. Do you mind joining us?"

"Thank you so much for the offer, Mrs Banda. I'd love to come with you, but I'm a bit occupied. I'm sorry."

She gazed at him, with a glum expression.

"Don't feel much offended, Mrs Banda. It's only that I'm on duty. If it'd not been so, I'd have joined you without any excuse.

"By the way, why do you prefer Clifford Kauri's hotel to other hotels?"

"It's our family's favourite hotel. Before Jacob died, he used to take us there most of the time. You get it?" She restored her smiling expression.

"I get it. That's fantastic. Have a good day and a blessed lunch too."

"Thanks, dear, but you've disappointed me. How could you turn down my offer just like that?" she complained disgustedly.

"Don't take yourself back to that, Eunice Banda. Haha. Don't worry, next time I won't dishonour the invitation, I promise."

The Banda family left the library. Although they had decided in the morning to lunch in the outlet where they had taken their breakfast, they suddenly changed their plans and proceeded to Kauri's Hotel, a very popular hotel with five stars, which belonged to Clifford Kauri.

Mrs Banda's attitude left the police detective with many questions. The woman seemed to have changed all of a sudden into an unreserved woman. She was no longer the lady everybody in the community had known for years, respected and recommended as an example of a down-to-earth woman.

From the hotel, the family drove to an orphanage called OCCO (Orphaned Child Caring Organisation). It was about five kilometres away from the city centre of Magamba. The place was built to shelter abandoned children and orphans. At the moment, there were about hundred children being taken care of by some retired Roman Catholic nuns.

Eunice reversed her car into a parking bay with a signpost bearing a capitalised inscription: REVERSE PARKING ONLY. She switched off the engine, and they got down. They went straight to the office of the principal. In the office, a plump woman dressed in a grey nun dress and an ashy veil was Sister Faith, the principal, seated on a swiveling chair behind a furnished mahogany desk. She looked up from her computer and shouted, "Wow! My best friend, you're welcome!" She stood up from the chair and danced towards her. They hugged and kissed each other.

"How're you, dear?" Eunice asked, removing her long hands from Faith's back to cease the hug.

"Fine, dear. I'm glad to see you again. Come and make yourself comfortable anywhere. The seats are all yours."

"Thank you."

"How're you, Sherry and Bob?"

"Very fine, Madam. Thank you for the seats."

"Don't mention it."

They chatted for a short time in the office and then walked out around the yard to see some developments on it. Some painters were doing an amazing job. All the buildings—except the public toilets—looked new. The ground was adorned with fascinating flowers and some green lawn.

All the OCCO children came together under a big tree near a soccer field and chatted with the Banda family.

"For the benefit of the new comers, this is Sherry Banda." Sister Faith gave some introductions. "I've always talked about her, and you've been eager to see who she is. She's the one whose father, Mr Banda, died some weeks ago. We're sorry for that.

"This girl is generous, well behaved and hardworking. I wish you'd copy from her.

"Today, she's brought you some loose biscuits. There're many packets of them. This means she loves you and cares about you.

"God bless you, Sherry."

"Thank you." Sherry clapped her hands slightly.

The children showed brilliant smiles on their faces, and they clapped their hands in return. As if that was not enough, they all rose and clustered around Sherry, cheering and hugging her.

Apart from expressing their abundant happiness and appreciation, they reserved some special time to show sympathies for the death of Mr Banda. They sang a song that brought much delight and comfort to the Banda family:

> There's a new home ahead of us;
> God's love will take us there.
> There's a new home ahead of you;
> God's love will take you there...

Sister Faith continued: "This is her mother, Eunice Banda. We've been friends for quite a long time since Sherry was a baby; that's if I'm not mistaken.

"This one, here, is Bob Banda, Sherry's brother. He supports his family's decisions that's why you see him here also. We thank you, Brother.

"Let's clap our hands for them all."

They applauded the family's love and unity. Sister Faith sent for the biscuits from her office and shared them equally. Everyone got their portion, ate and chatted for an hour, sharing jokes. After that, the family bid farewell, and the children gaped, waving at them as they walked away to their car. The waving stopped only when the vehicle was out of sight.

"Don't worry, my friends." Sister Faith comforted them. "They're gone, but not for good; they'll visit us again."

*

At around 3 p.m., all the detectives were in the office of DCI Nyoka. They had to give him some feedback before they knocked off duty. He had impatiently waited for that period to come; he wanted to find out whether the first move on Banda's case was according to his instructions or not, for he knew quite well that some of the detectives were opposing his mode of thought.

"Any leads?" DCI Nyoka folded his arms onto his chest. "Sergeant Green, present your results first!"

"Thank you, sir." He rose defiantly. "A few hours ago, I met Eunice Banda and her children in the 'Chat with Books' library. She told me that their favourite food outlets are Clifford Kauri's restaurant and his hotel. She added that those were the places Jacob Banda frequented. For that reason, I was convinced to suspect that he was most certainly poisoned in either of the two places. This is all I've at the moment, sir."

"Thanks." He nodded, smiling. "Next!"

Detective Constable Bere stood up. "Thank you, sir. I was at Bernard Bar; I got some information that he was last seen drinking beer at the same bar with some unidentified men before he was reported missing.

"Unfortunately, the informers failed to describe them."

"Well done," the officer in charge said cheerfully.

The last of them all was DC Francis. He had spent the whole day sleeping at his home, while his colleagues were working. He knew very well that Jacob Banda and DCI Nyoka were close friends, so he said, "I was at Bernard Hotel; the people I interviewed told me that they used to see him most of the time with you, sir."

Almost everyone laughed.

"Don't laugh at him," DCI Nyoka said, shaking his head. "Wonders never end. Anyway, I'm satisfied with your first move. Your leads are promising some good results. Keep it up. Finally, the truth will be revealed."

They were dismissed.

*

In the evening, Bomber and his gang were chatting in their rented room at Runyararo High Density in the western part of the city of Magamba. They surrounded a crate of opaque beer and some playing cards on a shabby wooden table positioned at the centre of the room. A big cigar of *mbanje* (marijuana) was making rounds, passing through their burnt lips. On the crude floor of the room, there were empty bottles, pieces of newspaper and cigar stubs scattered everywhere. The room had a permanent stench of stale cigarettes. Each of the gangsters, except Queen, had a knife in his pocket. As the men were smoking, the lady was sniffing some white powder and packing some of it into small plastic bags. There was reggae music playing at full blast.

"Motherfuckers!" Queen shouted. "You lost our chance of making money that day! You just let the bird fly away with all its feathers!"

Turning down the volume of the radio, Diesel admitted to it: "You're right, Queen! I even blamed myself for it; we're too slow to act!"

"Next time, we promise to do better!" said Planet.

"True!" Razor agreed.

"We need money, guys, for our food and for our drugs!" Bomber voiced.

"Let me go out, guys! The earliest bird catches the first worm!" Queen placed an empty plastic container of beer onto the table. "Be in touch, gang!" She put away what she had been packing and went to a small window, where she picked up her makeup kit and started applying some powder onto her face.

"All the best! Catch some really big fish, bitch!" Bomber cursed, his right arm wiping the empty beer container off the table.

"Okay, son of bitch!" she retorted, her right index finger vertically poking up into the air in front of Bomber's drunk-looking boned face.

Diesel, Planet and Razor laughed hysterically. All of a sudden, Bomber and Queen joined the laughter.

"Okay, it's enough! It's enough!" She stopped them, raising her voice. "Do you want to laugh until tomorrow?

"Let me go fishing now. I'm *gonna* be lucky to catch a dolphin. When it comes to this type of catch, I always need your support. Dolphins have much fat, so we need not miss the fat," she joked.

"It's obvious," Diesel voiced, "we're always ready to attack the dolphins and drain their fat. Once you get one, PM us."

"Bye." She waved her hand and left them.

There were already many ladies of the night loitering up and down the streets and around the nightclubs. She joined them.

An hour later, Bomber and his friends left their place. Razor carried a satchel with the packets of the white powder Queen had packed.

CHAPTER

5

IN the morning, Bob Banda sat facing DS Green in his office. Between them was a furnished desk with a tape recorder on it. DC Francis was standing at the door, which he had locked from the inside. Detective Constable Tilda leaned on the sill of a large open window, whose two long divided white lace curtains were partially closed to the extent that a speedy flying bat could pass between them untouched. She was scribbling something into her police diary; meanwhile, her workmates were firing questions and tape-recording everything.

"Mr Bob Banda"—DS Green stood up from his chair, staring at Bob—"the son of the late Jacob Banda, I say good morning once again."

"Morning, sir."

"I understand you're in your sound mind, aren't you?"

"Yes, I'm, sir." His heart was palpitating fast.

"Calm down. Don't be afraid. We're human beings like you. I'm the one who sent for you. We're here not to harass you but to gather evidence that'll lead us into arresting the criminals who killed your father and left you an orphan. I'm sure you get what I mean."

He nodded sadly.

"Be truthful in all your responses to our questions in order to make our work easier.

"If you lie to us, we'll charge you for deliberately supplying false information to public authority. It's a crime defined in the Criminal Law, Codification and Reform Act, Chapter 9 point 23. Understood?"

"Sir."

"You're our young brother. We worked very well with your father; therefore, we don't want to be hard on you. All we need is the truth."

Bob smiled. "Thank you, sir.

"May I have a chair with a cushion?"

DS Green shook his head: "Not now. Good things don't just come that way."

Bob drooped his head.

"Bob," he called and paused for some seconds, waiting for him to lift up his face, "when did you last see your national ID card?"

"It was in my wallet." He had some confidence. "But it got lost when I was at Matthew's home."

"When was that?" DC Francis motioned to look him in the eyes.

"Three weeks ago." He turned his face to him.

DS Green narrowed his eyes to him and demanded, "Give us the date!"

"Sorry, can't remember the date, but it was on Saturday during the night. The first Saturday of this month."

"Okay, and what were you doing during that time?"

"We're celebrating on a birthday party for Matthew's young sister." His left fingers were scratching his head.

"Did you inform anybody about your missing wallet?" DS Green walked to his chair, his eyes focused on Bob, and sat down.

"Yes, I announced it to everyone at the party."

"Did you report it to the police then?"

"No, I didn't."

"You should have made a police report."

"I'm sorry, I didn't think of that, sir."

"It's okay. Don't worry about it. I'm not offended at all." The sergeant paused and took his police diary and a pen from one of the desk drawers. "I see you're telling us the truth. So I'm giving you your wallet and the ID card through proper handover and takeover."

"Thank you, sir."

"Otherwise, how was the party? I wish I were invited." The sergeant smiled.

"It was very good." He smiled back. "Next time, we'll invite you, sir."

"How many people attended it?"

"Too many of them; I can't give you the actual figure, sir."

"May you give me the names of those you know who were at the party?" He was taking down every essential piece of information into his police diary.

He counted them, representing each of them with a finger: "D.J. Chinua; Mapamba, the comedian; Stanford; Matthew; Razor; Planet and Queen, the dancer. And many others."

"Okay, thanks, we'll come to you again for some more information when we need it."

Bob signed for his possessions and left the office.

During that time, Daniel Sango was in the Eden Forest again for the mission he disturbed the day he assisted Sherry to get out of the jungle. He was searching for his father's treasure, which got lost about 16 years ago when some unknown criminals murdered him. Nobody knew, except God, whether or not the treasure was still existing. Had it not been his father bothering him in his dreams, Daniel would not have dared the search. Although he was not faint-hearted, he—unlike his father—disliked forest adventures.

Contrary to many people's judgment on his slenderness, Daniel had strong bones—he was brave and determined, and nothing could easily scare him.

It's hot now, he thought, turning his face all around searchingly. *I need a place to rest.*

He had a haversack with some food on his back. In his right hand, he held a 303 rifle, and there was a catapult with its pebbles in one of his jacket pockets. On the right side of his waist, in a leather pouch, there was a knife. That armour belonged to his father. In the first time, Daniel had made a blunder to visit the Eden Forest without any weapon.

He trudged towards a leafy tree and skulked from the angry sun. The shade gave him some relief, but he was not that comfortable; his eyes ran cunningly from one thin branch to another, examining them carefully to find out if they were really parts of the tree. Having been satisfied with his examination, he unburdened himself and sat down. He took out his food from the haversack and enjoyed it, leaning on the tree trunk. That was his lunch of the day. After having it, he drifted off to sleep.

About a kilometre to the south of the tree lay a big rocky mountain with a traceable history of mysteries. Some centuries ago, the ancestors named it Mount Spirits, and none of the descendants dared to change the name.

As Daniel snored in his deep sleep, the weather changed suddenly. Some dark clouds formed from the mountain and spread quickly across the blue sky. The jungle became dark. When he woke up, he was astonished to see that some heavy rains were promising. He quickly picked up his goods and hurried around in search of a safe place to hide. Unfortunately, the rain caught him on the way, and he rushed back to where he was before. The leafy branches protected him from the downpour but never from the lightning. His bowel groaned every time the lightning streaked and the thunder rumbled. After some minutes, a fierce storm arose and added fuel to the fire. It came with an increase in the downpour and violated many tree branches and young plants. The rain began to reach him under the tree.

The hailstones hit the ground. The runoff percolated down into the streams leading into the Dead Gorge. The potholes and the pits were filled up with stagnant water, and frogs blew trumpets of joy. Dead leaves tendered a pungent smell. The trees shook violently as the gale hit against them. Their branches broke off, and some of their fresh leaves were dispersed.

An hour later, the storm and the rain stopped; that was after they had caused a lot of damage to the jungle. Daniel could not continue with his mission, so he moved away and looked for a safe place to spend the coming night. After searching for the place for some time without positive results, he sat down on a rock, tired. He thought of going back home, but it was too late for that. As he lifted up his face and cast his eyes at distant areas, he noted a baobab tree and hoped to find a hollow in it. He got up and walked to it. The massive tree had a warm cave. He crouched in, holding a torch in his left hand. The place was empty and clean. A brilliant smile tore his lips, but it did not last long. It immediately vanished when he began to associate the cave with the one in which he had once encountered a fierce snake.

Trying to get rid of the disturbing memories of the past adventure with the snake, he fished out a cigarette from his breast pocket and planted it between his trembling lips. He lit it. As he took it, a cloud of smoke broke into tiny grey shreds, which circulated randomly in the poorly ventilated room. Suddenly came eerie sounds from Mount Spirits. Daniel's heart skipped. They sounded like the voices of the children and the adults blustering. The noise continued for some time; it seemed as if there were people fighting.

Daniel stood up facing the entrance and exit. His back and his shaking hands grappled the wall. He suddenly caught sight of a transparent human figure walking past the opening. The figure walked right round the baobab tree and reappeared at the opening. It was a lady dressed in a white garment. Daniel concluded that it was a ghost. He was right; that was Gertrude Jena's ghost.

Daniel remembered a Southern-African belief that ghosts get offended when they are openly insulted and reminded that the person they are haunting is not responsible for their deaths. The belief caused the fear to disappear from him. He grabbed his 303 rifle and tried to shoot the ghost, but when he pressed the trigger, hot water poured out instead of a bullet. Angrily, he cursed the ghost, and it disappeared.

After the encounter with Gertrude's ghost, he saw a bus halt about 100 metres away from the baobab. Its passengers had pale skin and were in white garments. Their noses and their twinkling eyes were unique. All of them, except the driver, got off and started running right round the bus. They were following behind one another. After doing so for a short time, they reboarded the bus and disappeared.

What's going on? Daniel shook his head, perplexed. *Are they the ghosts of those people who died in that bus accident some years ago?*

The rumour still spreads that the accident was caused by Gertrude's ghost. I think these ghosts are after it. Yes, that's it.

I caused nobody's death; let me relax.

The rest of the night, he slept well despite that there was no comfort on the crude floor.

In the morning, just before the sunrise, a chill in the air aroused him from sleep. He wiped his eyes and exited the cave, carrying his possessions. He slouched towards the south, searching for his father's treasure.

Right ahead of him, he spotted a fruit tree and trotted towards it. The tree was unfamiliar, but its dark-brown fruits round in shape looked edible. Daniel plucked one and tasted it. He threw away his possessions and hopped around, singing and dancing. It came at the right time when he had exhausted all his food.

His height allowed him to start eating the fruits he could reach from the ground. Later, when he had had enough of them, he vigorously shook the tree and caused more fruits to fall down. He raked them together and collected them into his haversack; then, he picked up the other belongings and walked east.

Now, the sun was above the eastern horizon, and it beamed so brightly he had to cap his face with a hand to see clearly. Just a few metres to the southeast, he saw a green faux leather bag lying under a thorny bush. His face lightened up with excitement, perhaps, of discovering what he was looking for. He ran to it. The expression on his face changed when he saw a snaking track of gregarious ants prowling tiny chunks of minced meat from the bag to an anthill embedded close by. A disturbed swarm of greenflies was buzzing around. He suspected that it was a dumped baby, so he decided to report it to the police.

He used his white t-shirt to mark the scene and walked away. As he hurried to the main road, he found a pair of pink lady's shoes left about 20 metres away from the bag. One of them had some dry blood on it. He did not touch them—he just made a note in his mind and proceeded with his journey through the thickets. It was a long walk to the road.

"I'm disturbed every time I come here," he complained.

After some time, he reached the main road and found the taxi that once gave him a lift when he was with Sherry. The driver and her attire were the same. That startled him. "We meet again?" He opened the door.

"Yes, of course." The driver smirked. "This is my registered route.

"Anyway, what's your business in this place? Last time, I picked you up around here."

"Hmm, it's a long story. I'm looking for my father's treasure. He lost it in this jungle about 16 years ago."

"And you think you can find it after such a long period?" She cackled, looking at him.

Daniel scowled and did not say anything of that sort to her again.

Within a few minutes, they had reached the city centre. Daniel sighed with relief that he had arrived safely.

"How much?" He dipped his left hand into his jacket pocket.

"You pay me next time." She left.

He stared at the car, openmouthed, as it sped off in the other direction.

*

"A Sierra-Delta-Delta scene again," Constable Mururi, a DUB police officer, commented as he joined the team attending a fresh scene reported by Daniel. "Another sudden death. Somebody here uses a charm that attracts serious cases. The person is getting us busy all the time. Recently, it was Jacob Banda's body. This time I don't know whose body it is. Let's go and see it."

Nobody responded to his weird comments.

When the police officers reached the jungle, they searched for the scene point and quickly noticed Daniel's white t-shirt, which he had used as an indicator. The helicopter landed. The detectives jumped out and marched to the scene in a single file. As they approached the thick bush, they noticed the green bag, which lay beneath it. An unpleasant smell welcomed them, and a swarm of greenflies honoured their arrival. Detective Constable Tilda carefully pulled the bag to an open space, where she cut it open. The smell increased, and the flies that had dispersed buzzed back in large numbers. DC Francis broke a leafy branch off the bush and swatted them off the dead body of an albino baby boy, whose back had been mercilessly masticated by the ants.

Daniel whispered something into Detective Sergeant Green Ash's right ear, and he led him to the place where he had seen the pink shoes of a lady.

Having pegged and photographed every point of police interest, the detectives carefully packed the corpse into a body bag and the pink shoes into an exhibit bag. They departed from the Eden Forest and flew straight to the mortuary of Magamba General Hospital.

*

At the police station, DS Green sat in DCI Nyoka's office.

"It's an albino baby boy," DS Green said. "We found him in a green faux leather bag. The bag was placed beneath a thick bush. About 20 metres away from the bush, we picked up a pair of pink shoes. Lady's shoes."

"Shame"—Detective Chief Inspector Nyoka commiserated—"So what's your decision?"

"I think we should sit down with Sherry. She may help us track the men who kidnapped her. I suspect they're the ones who killed that baby, perhaps, on a different day."

DCI Nyoka mused on his subordinate's suggestion and then said, "Your suggestion is good, and your idea is bright, but caution is needed. I'll be directing you in every step. Don't ask a lot to vex her. She's not a criminal but just an ordinary person to assist us."

"Sir, I promise that my team and I'll work according to your instructions."

"Okay. So far I'm pleased with your progress, Green. Keep it up with your guys." He paused. "Has a docket been compiled?"

"It's being compiled in the charge office right now."

"Okay, that's good." He looked at his wall watch. "After work, I'll pass through Sherry's home and ask her to visit my office so we can ask her to help us track down these kidnappers. Is that okay?"

"Very okay, sir."

"But for the next two days, she'll be very busy. So we can meet her after two days."

"That's alright, sir."

"Did you correctly label the corpse?" He gazed at him, with narrowed eyes.

"Yes, sir." He opened his police diary. "It's labeled B235411P, and it's in the Infants Mortuary No: 03."

"Thank you." He copied the information down.

CHAPTER
6

THREE days later, Detective Sergeant Green Ash was working in his office when DCI Nyoka just came in, patting on his pockets confusedly. He was murmuring and looking around searchingly. DS Green said nothing but just stared at him. He left the office in what appeared to be a weird hurry. Along the corridor, he came across Superintendent Edwards. The short man was the superintendent in charge of crime management; he halted promptly, adjusted his spectacles and gaped at DCI Nyoka as he was playacting like a madman. He followed him into his office to ask if there was anything wrong.

"Good afternoon, sir," DCI Nyoka said.

"It's still early in the morning, Detective Chief Inspector Nyoka." Detective Supt Edwards glanced at his wristwatch. "Are you okay? You didn't even greet me when you saw me outside."

"Sorry, sir."

"Are you okay?"

He nodded: "Yes, sir."

"Yes?" Edwards chuckled. "You can't say yes because you look like someone troubled."

"I'm just searching for my cellphone, sir."

"Just a cellphone? You're not serious, man." Supt Edwards laughed. "It seems as if you've lost something bigger than that.

"Anyway, let me take this opportunity to let you know there is an urgent meeting for all the officers in charge of the CID Homicide in this province. The venue is the PHQ conference room. We're going to have noble ranks from PGHQ. So we need to go like now and prepare for them."

"Thank you, sir." He piled up some papers on his desk. "What about my cellphone?"

"Cellphones are important, I know, but not to the extent of making you behave like this. Why are you too concerned about it? I'm surprised."

"You can't understand it, sir. Anyway, let's go." He wiped off tiny drops of sweat that had formed on his forehead.

The two left Magamba CID Station and took a ride to the Provincial Headquarters located about 30 kilometres away from their station.

An hour later, Sherry Banda knocked on the door of DS Green's office. She was wearing a red miniskirt and a white bodice. Her feet were in white sandals, and her right toe was in a white bandage.

"Come in!" DS Green called, looking at the door.

She stepped in, turned her back to him and closed the door. Then, she faced him again, walked and stopped right in front of him like someone practising for a modelling show. "Hi." She looked at him, with half-closed eyes.

"Hi." He glanced at her face.

"Is your boss around? I tried his cellphone number, but it's not reachable."

"I'm sorry, I have many bosses, but if you mean Mr Nyoka, he's just gone out for a meeting."

"Okay." Some of her right fingers were tilting her eyebrows. "He informed me that you need my help to track the kidnappers; is that so?"

"Correct."

"He also said you must question me in his presence. So at what time will he be back?" She was now pushing her hair backwards.

"Sit down, lady!" DC Tilda shouted after opening the door. "We can question you even without him!"

Sherry sat down sheepishly and wondered how the lady had got in. She had not heard any sound of the door opening.

She looked her in the eyes. "It's over. Don't ever think like that again. Don't let anyone fool you that we have no power to question you without them."

DS Green called DC Francis, and the three started interrogating her. On the right side of the desk, close to where Sherry was seated with her hands crossed on her thighs, there was the tape recorder, which the detectives had once used to record Bob. DC Tilda was now by the window, staring at her. DC Francis had papers and a pen on a clipboard; it showed that he was ready to record some important information. It dawned on her that the detectives had not called her for the case of the kidnappers. The door had been locked from the inside, and the curtains had been closed. It all baffled her. She tried to conceal her shivering, but it was impossible to get rid of it.

"Don't be afraid, Sherry," DS Green said. "We just need some information from you. Feel free."

She nodded without parting her lips.

"Are you married?"

"No."

"Do you have or did you have a baby out of wedlock?"

She remained silent.

DC Tilda pointed at her breasts. "Your breasts show they're sucked."

Sherry drooped her head.

"Look up!" DC Francis shouted. "And answer the questions! Don't take us for fools!"

"I... I... I never had one."

Sergeant Green stood up and walked to her. "What happened to your toe?" He pointed his finger at it. "I can see it's bandaged."

"I got injured in the Eden Forest when I was escaping from the kidnappers," she said, looking at the toe.

DC Tilda chipped in: "How many were they?"

"Four." She drooped her head again.

"Whenever you answer me, you look straight into my eyes, understood?"

She nodded.

DS Green took a deep breath and blew into his hands. He walked to his chair and sat down. After a while, he pulled out one of the desk drawers and took out a pair of pink shoes wrapped in a khaki cover. He placed it onto the desk and glanced at Sherry. When he removed the cover, her heart skipped.

"I believe they're yours. One of them has blood from your toe."

"Yes, sir, they're mine. They got lost in the Eden Forest."

"Okay." He opened another drawer and fished out a khaki envelope with three snaps. He pulled the snaps out and handed them over to her. "Did you see anything like this in the Eden Forest?"

She looked at them but did not say a thing. Tears formed in her eyes.

"I repeat, did you see anything like this in the Eden Forest?"

"No." She shook her head. "I didn't see it."

He frowned. "We found your shoes near this bag with the corpse of an albino baby; therefore, we—"

There was a knock. DC Francis opened the door and then backed off. DCI Nyoka walked in and foamed at the mouth when he saw Sherry among them.

"What the hell are you doing with this young lady?" He looked all around the office.

"She's giving us the descriptions of the kidnappers, sir," said Detective Constable Tilda.

"Shut up! I'm not talking to you! I only talk with your senior!" He turned to Detective Sergeant Green. "Bring that tape recorder to me!"

DS Green pushed the tape recorder to him and relaxed on his chair, biting his lips.

DCI Nyoka played it and rubbed off the recording. "What kind of police officers are you? Why are you so barbaric? Didn't I instruct you to do it when I'm with you? You've refused to follow my lawful instructions; I'm going to charge you for that! You deserve disciplinary action! If you're not careful, you'll lose your job!

"You don't really know this police organisation, do you? Don't just put yourself into risks. This organisation won't stand with you when you're in trouble.

"By ignoring some things, you won't lose anything. Consider your safety first, stupid idiots! Who're you in this big organisation? I'm sorry for you. How much does it pay you?

"As for you, Detective Sergeant Green Ash, I'm going to process papers for your immediate transfer! You're not worth to be in this section!

"If you're not careful, you'll lose your job! Your family will suffer simply because of your foolishness! Why do you waste your time on useless things? Don't you have better things to do? I'm sorry for you. Learn to reason like an adult!"

"Sorry, sir."

"Sir"—DC Tilda complained—"what you're doing isn't fair. This discourages us a lot. You can't reprove your subordinates in front of Sherry, a civilian person. This isn't good at all."

"How dare you talk to your superior like that?" DCI Nyoka pointed at her, his finger trembling. "Don't you know who I am? I'm your boss!"

"Tilda"—DS Green chipped in—"mind your speech. Leave this office."

"No! This is too much, Serge! I'm not desperate; I can quit this fucked-up career! This man is ill-treating us, as though we're his slaves, yet we're his workmates. You lack professionalism, Mr Boss." She strode out of the office. Sherry also left it, but on her own.

"Green, did you hear what she's just said? Anyway, we'll see who'll fall to the ground. All of you are in trouble." After glancing at his wristwatch, he strutted out and closed the door with a bang, which left the sergeant and his subordinate, DC Francis, gaping.

*

At Golden, the low density suburb where Clifford Kauri lived, there was the Mpofu family with an albino baby boy, whom they always left with a maid whenever they were travelling out of the country on business. In the evening, they returned home and found their maid, Thandiwe, shedding tears on her bed. The window of her room was broken.

Mrs Mpofu turned around, searching for her boy. "Where's Nathan?" Her instincts had told her that something was wrong with him.

The maid blubbered: "Kidnapped... He—"

"What? Be clear!" She grabbed her, now crying, and dragged her to the floor.

"Don't do that, honey." Mr Mpofu intervened and pulled his wife back. Thandiwe got up and ran onto the bed, where she covered herself with the blankets.

"Leave me alone, Mpofu! I need my son!" She twisted her husband's hand and pushed him away; then, she dived onto the bed and started striking Thandiwe. The husband staggered up from the floor and rescued the maid. He escorted her out of the house, whilst his wife was hurling objects at them. They hurried to a car parked outside and drove away to the OCCO centre.

In Sister Faith's office, Thandiwe explained how Nathan was kidnapped.

Sister Faith said, looking Mr Mpofu in the eyes, "The police said they found the baby; I got this from a newspaper."

"Are you sure?"

"Yes, Mr Mpofu. Right now, go to Magamba Police Station."

"Thank you." He stood up hastily. "Please, look after Thandi. I'll be back for her."

"She's in safe hands; don't worry."

He arrived at the police station, where he was directed to see Detective Chief Inspector Nyoka in his office.

"Mr Mpofu," DCI Nyoka said, "Sister Faith told you the truth; we did find the baby, but he was already dead."

Mr Mpofu wept bitterly.

He allowed him to weep until he was composed. Then, he continued: "As I speak right now, he's in the mortuary. We have been waiting for any of his relatives to show up so we'd carry out the required postmortem in their presence.

"Calm down, Mr Mpofu. I'm sorry for this unexpected loss. On behalf of my section members, we promise to apprehend any culprit who committed this crime.

"A similar incident happened last week. Some men kidnapped a lady by the name Sherry Banda and tried to kill her in the Eden Forest. Thank God, she managed to escape from them. I suspect those men are the ones who kidnapped and murdered your son.

"Anyway, can you explain to me how it happened?"

Mr Mpofu was sobbing.

"Come on, be a gentleman, Mr Mpofu. Just accept the misfortune. Death is for all. We'll all die. Every situation is predetermined."

"How's my wife going to cope with it?"

"That's something else, my man." He sneered. "Look!" He pointed at a watch on the wall behind Mr Mpofu. "It's now 6 p.m. I ought to have knocked off duty at exactly half past 4. I have a home; I don't sleep here, Mister.

"Instead of helping me with the information I need to arrest the criminals, you're busy moaning. Didn't I give you enough time to weep? If you were a woman, I'd be patient."

"I'm sorry."

"Yah. Now," he demanded, "tell me; what happened?"

"Our maid left the baby asleep in the house and went outside to attend a visitor, who delayed her for some minutes. When she came back, she discovered that the baby was missing and the window had been smashed."

"Shame. This is pathetic. Why didn't you report it the very day?"

"We were out of the country on business."

"Where's your maid?"

"I drove her to the OCCO centre for safety. My wife had got mad at her after hearing the news."

"You did a wise thing, Mr Mpofu." He clapped his hands slightly. "Was the visitor a man?"

"A lady, she said."

"Anyway, we'll record much information from your maid." He looked at the wall watch. "Now, you can go home and come back with your wife tomorrow in the morning. Together, we'll go to the mortuary. Don't forget to bring your national ID card, the baby's birth cards and other relevant documents."

He nodded.

"Don't be too worried, my good friend. This is life. Death is for every living thing on earth."

"Thank you, sir."

"In the case of your wife, you should find one or two female counsellors with whom you can approach her tonight."

"Thank you." He left the office.

*

The following day, two female OCCO counsellors sat with Mr and Mrs Mpofu in DCI Nyoka's office.

"With the documents you've brought here, we'll verify whether or not the baby is yours." DCI Nyoka stood up from his chair. "Let me call two of my detectives to accompany us to the mortuary." He walked out to Detective Sergeant Green's office, where he bragged in front of him: "The parents of that dumped baby are in my office right now. I'm taking them to the mortuary right away to identify the body. Only Detective Constable Bere and Detective Constable Samson, that new detective on probation, are to accompany me. We'll have two uniformed police officers from the charge office.

"The body will go through postmortem tomorrow. The same detectives I'm going with today are the ones I'll go with tomorrow. Understood?"

"It's okay," he replied wryly. *Who cares?*

"I'll brief you, clever detective, on the postmortem results. Maybe that'll make you handle Sherry better than what you're doing right now." He sneered, left the office and slammed the door.

At around 10 a.m., a mortuary attendant led Nathan's parents, the OCCO counsellors, two uniformed police officers and three detectives into the infants' mortuary. Mr and Mrs Mpofu whimpered as they sighted Nathan's dead body labelled B235411P.

The doctors conducted the postmortem on the same day. The results were that the baby had succumbed to suffocation due to strangulation.

"Hey!" DCI Nyoka whined. "These heartless criminals throttled this innocent boy to death! What the hell did they do that for?"

"This is really bad," one of the counsellors commented.

Arrangements to cremate the body were made.

*

At the police station, in DS Green's office, DC Francis was complaining about the officer in charge: "I'll quit this job, Serge. I can't stand this tyrannical superior. It's better I find another job."

DS Green shook his head. "Don't say that again, Francis. Learn to deal with all characters in life. Even if you get another job, expect to meet the same type."

"This one is too much, Serge."

"Be strong. This will be over soon. It's just a matter of time. Sometimes, pressure comes our way just to take us up to a better level."

"You see? Here's the pressure to take me to another job."

"There's one thing I observed. When you see your subordinates or employees advancing themselves academically, while they're still working for you, it clearly means they're preparing either for promotions or to quit their current jobs. Once you observe this, you should work to put your house in order. Failure to do so... Haha."

"Haha! This is true; I started my diploma last year, intending to quit the police."

*

A day after the postmortem, the detectives thronged DCI Nyoka's office for a short caucus.

"Good morning, ladies and gentlemen," DCI Nyoka greeted them, with a smile that seemed to tear his oily lips into shreds.

"Morning, sir," the detectives chorused.

He cleared his throat. "I've a special announcement to make to you today. It's all about the leads we now have pertaining to the outstanding cases we've been working on tirelessly. It's not so necessary we may need to start the meeting with an opening prayer. Allow me to go straight to the core business.

"Yesterday, we attended and witnessed the postmortem on the albino body we found in the Eden Forest. The results showed the baby died due to suffocation. He was throttled to death.

"The accused persons kidnapped him while he was in the custody of a babysitter whose name is Thandiwe. This girl was employed by Peter Mpofu from the Orphaned Child Caring Organisation. She's an orphan herself and is 20 years old.

"I instruct you to question her. She has got something to tell us. Don't intimidate her like what you did to Sherry, an innocent person. Learn to use tactic skills when investigating cases.

"I warn you not to implicate the Banda family into these cases, understood?"

"Yes, sir." Not all of them answered.

"Those are mere complainants like anyone else." He added: "Every complainant is our valuable client. Treat them with respect and dignity, and give them high quality service. Don't harass them."

Some of the subordinates agreed.

"I'm here also to let you know that my vac. leave is starting next week. DS Green will be the member in charge; this is just for a month during my absence. Very soon, Detective Inspector Kayala and Detective Assistant Inspector Kwenda, who're both on their vac. leaves, will join you. In spite of their presence, I'll be visiting your offices to check progress." He paused for some seconds. "You get it?"

"Sir."

"Any questions?"

DS Green raised his hand. "Where exactly do we get Thandiwe?"

He scorned: "Wasn't it clear enough for a baby to understand? Didn't I mention the OCCO centre? Learn not to focus on issues that are not important when you're in a serious meeting like this."

"Thank you, sir." DS Green slouched back on his chair.

After the meeting, they were deployed to cover areas of interest.

DS Green, DC Tilda and DC Francis drove to a large recreational park on the outskirts of the city. The place was a paradise fragment on earth. At the centre, it had a beautiful runway for small planes.

While DS Green's colleagues were making fun, taking photos of themselves, he was seated on a steel chair, deliberating on Clifford's men and their green biplane landed at the centre of the park. One of the men, their leader, whose first name was Gilbert, was seated with a familiar lady between two bushy flowers; meanwhile, his friends were on the biplane.

A recollection clicked DS Green's mind: The biplane was tainted to him. He had seen it making one or two trips to and fro the direction of the Eden Forest almost every year. So he was curious to know whether or not the jungle was its destination. If it was really its destination, what could be its business in it all the time?

He could imagine those men kidnapping Jacob Banda and the albino baby into the jungle, using that biplane. He linked them to every case that had occurred in the Eden Forest and suspected that Jacob might have eaten the poisoned food from any of Clifford's food outlets.

It was possible, as he thought, for Clifford with his men to kidnap Nathan Mpofu because he lived in the same residential area with the boy's parents—they were neighbours. The detective wanted so much to question the men, but he hesitated because of his superior, DCI Nyoka, who was their closest friend that was very good at defeating the course of justice and abusing his office—he was always standing as a lawyer for his friends and their relatives.

When he was busy digesting those things in his mind, his subordinates were mischievously zooming and taking photos and short videos of Gilbert and the lady, who had gone out of control and begun to kiss and caress each other.

Out of the blue, two women, who looked annoyed, strode towards them from behind.

"Gilbert! What're you doing here?" one of them yelled angrily. She started beating both of them. "Why are you cheating on me? What do I lack to satisfy you, hubby? Tell me!" She was shouting at the top of her voice.

"Stop it!" The other woman tried to refrain her.

"Leave me alone!" She pushed her away.

"Please, stop it," she cried.

"Who's this junky prostitute?" She shook Gilbert by the collar.

"She's Queen; we work together. It's not what you think. Don't do this, please."

The security personnel of the place came to intervene. By then, many spectators had already surrounded them, taking pictures and recording videos. The three were taken to a guardroom. DC Tilda followed them and pretended as if she was a witness.

After a short time, Gilbert shambled out of the room to the biplane, facing down. A two-hundred-metre distance became a two-hundred-kilometre one. He could not manage a thousand eyes from different people around him. He felt to have lost all his dignity. Fortunately, his colleagues got down to meet him, and they shielded him all the way to the biplane. Quickly, they flew away, but the videos and the pictures had already been taken.

A few minutes later, DC Tilda and Queen came out, holding cellphones. They exchanged contact numbers.

Gilbert's wife was released soon after Queen had left the place.

CHAPTER

7

AT Mr Mpofu's residence, the detectives completed their scene investigations and greenlit the family to use the place. They only managed to pick up a scratched airtime card at the scene.

*

From the recreational park, DS Green, DC Francis and DC Tilda drove to a residential location where Matthew, one of Bob Banda's best friends, lived. When they reached the place, they found him available with Stanford, his closest friend who was also a friend to Bob.

"Hi, guys," DS Green greeted them, trying to be friendly.

"Hi," Mathew answered, a wave of a wan smile on his lips.

"I'm Detective Sergeant Green Ash." He showed them his police ID card. "With me here, eh, are Detective Constable Francis and Detective Constable Tilda." He was pointing at them one by one.

"Okay." The boys' bowels began to complain.

"Yeah." DC Francis smirked.

"May I visit the toilet, sir?" Matthew pressed his buttocks with his hands.

"Hmm, me too." Stanford moved around, as though he was looking for a way to escape.

"No, don't be afraid." DS Green raised his hand halfway. "We're here only for Bob's lost wallet. He said it got lost here. Is it true?"

DC Tilda added: "During your sister's birthday party."

Matthew sighed and shook his head. "It's a lie; he didn't lose anything here."

Stanford just nodded nervously.

"Where did he lose it then?" DC Francis advanced to them.

"We don't know." They backed off shortly.

"Anyway"—DS Green chipped in—"thanks for your help, boys. Next time, we'll call you for written statements to support yourselves. We don't want a bad situation whereby you end up being victims. You look very innocent, I see.

"By the way, who were the dancers for your party?"

"Only Queen," Stanford said.

"Wow, I missed it. Right, guys, have a good day. Like I said, we'll call you for some statements. Any time from now. Good bye."

"Thank you, sir." They looked at one another.

The detectives proceeded to the Orphaned Child Caring Organisation centre to interview Thandiwe concerning the kidnapping and the subsequent murder of Nathan Mpofu.

At the OCCO centre, they got the chance to talk with Thandiwe.

"Thanks, Thandiwe," DS Green said warmly after some introductions. "May you explain to us how it happened?"

She prepared her gullet. "I was sweeping the yard; meanwhile, Nathan was asleep in my room. During that time, a certain lady selling clothes knocked on the main gate, and I attended her. Outside the durawall, she took my time... Minutes later, she left in a hurry when her cellphone had rung. After sometime, I went into the house, and I was shocked to see that the baby was missing and the window had been broken."

"Umm." DC Tilda shook her head. "What time and date did all that happen?"

"At around 3 p.m., but I forget the date."

"Don't be ridiculous." She chuckled. "You forget the date? Anyway, we'll have it from our papers."

DC Francis asked, "Was the gate locked?"

"No."

"What time was it when the lady's cellphone rang?" Sergeant Green was writing down in his police diary everything Thandiwe was saying.

"I'm not quite sure, but it's between 3 p.m. and half past 3."

DC Tilda asked, "Didn't you hear any sound of the window being broken?"

"I heard it, but the lady concluded that it was from our neighbours."

"If you see the lady anywhere," she asked, taking a camera from her handbag, "will you be able to identify her?"

"Yes, I'll."

"Here, I've got some pictures in my camera." She turned the camera on to view Gilbert's and Queen's photos. She showed them to her.

Thandiwe's face lightened up, and she quickly inclined her head up and down: "Yes, this is the lady!"

"What about this man?" She pointed her finger at Gilbert's image. "Have you ever met him anywhere?"

"No." She shook her head. "He's a stranger."

"Okay. Thank you, Thandi. One day we'll call you to identify her if she's linked to this crime, right?"

"Thank you."

The detectives bid farewell to the OCCO principal and her staff members.

*

One week later, soon after DCI Nyoka's vac. leave had started, the member in charge, Detective Sergeant Green Ash, told Matthew and Stanford to come to his office. The boys woke up as early as before the sunrise and waited for him at the police station. They huddled under a mango tree. Here and there, they were rubbing their palms together to warm their numbed fingers. The worst part of it was that none of the police officers on duty considered them, except the one holding a rifle at the main gate, who had asked them why they had visited the police station at that time. That was all from him.

At around 7.40 a.m., DS Green reached the police station and parked his car. He got out and walked towards Stanford and Matthew, who—though with hard smiles on their faces—greeted him.

"Hi, guys," he greeted them back. "See me at exactly 20 past 8. Now I'm rushing for a morning parade."

"Okay, sir. Thank you so much. Thank you. Thank you, sir." They hung around, basking in the new sun. The mist had just disappeared, and the sun was clearing goose pimples off their skin.

Having deployed the other detectives to cover the area, the member in charge called DC Francis and DC Tilda to his office and briefed them on how they were going to handle the two boys. DC Tilda got plain papers, a pen and a clipboard. DC Francis took two metal chairs with no cushions and positioned them in one of the corners. DS Green set the tape recorder on the desk.

At exactly 8.20 a.m., the boys knocked on the door and were called in. They stood in front of the desk and gawked at DS Green, who directed them to the metal chairs in the corner. Before they moved their feet, they looked at the chairs and then back at him. When they noticed his contorted look, they walked to them and sat down.

"Boys"—the sergeant said, an unfriendly look on his face—"we don't want you to waste our time. I think you can see by yourselves that the setup in our office isn't for a joke. Take time to look around."

The boys turned their nervous faces around.

"Anyway, don't be afraid, but be truthful; just that." He stood up. "Only the truth will set you free. If you avoid it, you'll put yourselves in danger.

"Now, tell us. Where's Bob's wallet?"

"We don't know, sir."

"Don't pretend as if you know nothing about it! Bob lost his wallet at your home, Matthew! We just need to bring the wallet back to him; there's no biggie. Bob's national ID card was in that wallet, and he wants to use it to apply for his late father's pension-contribution refunds. So give back the wallet."

"Nothing—"

"Shut up!" DC Francis charged towards them and pushed them onto the floor. "I'll kill you today! Don't waste our time here! This is a serious case, and it's not only about the wallet!

"Remember you were all drunk that's why you forget about it! However, I'll force you to remember everything! I'm going to do it today, not tomorrow!"

"Sir, we were drunk, but we knew what we were doing," Matthew said pitiably.

"If you knew, why then would you forget Bob's wallet?"

"There was enough light, sir," Matthew said. "We'd—"

"Shut up! 'We'd... we'd...' what?" DC Francis parodied his words. "You took advantage of your 'enough light' to spot and hide the wallet! You're still joking, morons! This is just the beginning; the end will come! Before the end comes, there's going to be breathing of fire and gnashing of teeth, particularly from you!"

"Take them to the interrogation room!" Sergeant Green commanded, creases of anger on his forehead.

The boys were dragged out in handcuffs to a room where there was darkness, which overpowered two little lights fixed above two other metal chairs. The poor lights only shone onto the smallest part where they were forced to sit. The huge room had sticky liquid like polish smeared on its floor. The stuff reeked of a heavy odour that required someone, for health sake, to use respirators or to cover their noses with palms or a piece of cloth. Coming from the eastern side of the room—maybe from the outside—was an eerie sound; it was not too loud, but it just irritated and disturbed ears.

Is that a workshop? Matthew's mind was whirling. *These metal chairs, I'm sure, are manufactured from that damn side.*

"You'll stay here until you decide to tell us the truth! Also know this smell is from a mixture of a strange floor polish and the blood of some suspects who perished in this place! This is food for thought!" DC Francis slammed the door, locked it and switched off the dim lights from the outside. The room became more horrible to them.

Matthew contorted his face. "Pew. Disgusting. So our bare feet are in contact with the blood of other people who're tortured here?"

"There is a cobbler I know who operates near my father's shop," Stanford said in a low voice full of fear.

"So what?" Matthew asked curiously.

"I suggest we admit to taking Bob's wallet. When we get home, we see the cobbler and ask him to make it for us. And we take it to Bob. Isn't this simple?"

"Simple as you think like a kid, Stan. What about the ID card in question? What if it was used somewhere for illegal deals? How would you know? The moment you begin to accept that you know something about it, it means you're involved, and you'll be in for it."

Enlightened, Stanford nodded. Had Matthew not been controlling him several times, he would have been blurting out a lot, for he was a faint-hearted boy who could not walk alone through the dark. It was a big risk to involve him in any secret or illicit deal.

Thirty minutes later, the door was opened. They heard audible footsteps of more than one person entering the room, but they could not make out anyone. The room was in pitchy darkness. Suddenly, there was a sound similar to that of a knife being sharpened. The door was slammed again, and the sharpening sound ceased. There was some horrific silence for a few minutes. Stanford sobbed.

DS Green and DC Francis opened the door, switched on the little lights and stepped in.

"Now," DS Green said, "we're releasing you to your homes on one condition. You tell us the truth about Bob's wallet."

"There's nothing to tell more than what we've already told you, sir," Matthew said.

DS Green shook his head. "That's not the truth. For now, go home. We'll call you again. So far we're giving you enough time to make your final decision to tell us the truth.

"Francis, get them out."

The boys were released, and they hired a taxi to the most beautiful recreational park on the outskirts of the town. There, they digested their experience with the police and wondered why Bob had filed the allegation against them; after all, they had been loyal to him and his family for years.

Matthew turned to his friend. "How can Bob do this? Why does he want to betray us? What's he really up to?"

"The only way I can relieve myself is to expose Bob's family," Stanford said rebelliously.

Matthew's heart skipped. "How?"

Stan looked down.

"Be careful not to set the snare that'll trap you.

"Hey, Stan, look up at them." He pointed his shaking finger at Bob's mother and Officer Nyoka. "What're they doing here?"

Stan raised his head and saw them flirting near a rose plant at the eastern end of the recreational park. "That's the man behind everything. He's the one advising Bob to report against us. I hate him."

"I don't think so."

"This is the truth, dude. You don't know anything. Wake up.

"Are they now married?"

"No, they're not, but they're in love. After the death of her husband, her behaviour suddenly changed. These days, she acts like a prostitute. Officer Nyoka is really driving her crazy."

The two flirted in the recreational park like Adam and Eve making it in the Garden of Eden. For some time, they had been trying to conceal it from the limelight, but love acts in a crazy way—they failed it.

"Matthew, do you know they started this before Mr Banda died?"

Matthew laughed. "You're blurting out lies now."

"It's true; I'm serious."

"I know you very well, Stan. You sometimes just say things without careful consideration. What exactly is your problem? I'm afraid of you. You're likely to say anything when the police call us again."

Stanford remained silent. An old man laughs not at ease when dry bones are mentioned in a proverb. Matthew had touched his real weakness.

DCI Nyoka and his partner rose up, straightened their clothes and left the rose plant. They strolled towards the west, where administration offices of the park were situated.

They held each other by the waists. On their way, they met Clifford Kauri coming from the offices. In his right hand, he held a brown briefcase, which matched his point shoes.

"Ah!" DCI Nyoka halted in front of him. "What a humble millionaire! You're also found in places like this?"

"Yes, my dear," Clifford said cheerfully, "but once in a blue moon. I'm here for a short outdoor caucus with my local men."

"That's wonderful. Unfortunately, you've found me already leaving. See you some other time."

"No problem, my brother. Hmm, may you spare me a minute of your time?" Clifford plucked a wad of banknotes from his briefcase. "Take this little, and buy yourself some lunch."

"Thanks a lot. You've made my day, pal. Thank you once again. Be blessed."

"You're welcome, sir. You deserve more than this, boss, because you protect us in this city. Without you, we're doomed."

The two lovers parted ways with Clifford and proceeded to the administration offices.

Matthew and Stanford grasped it all. Like what many other people in the city of Magamba supposed, the boys suspected that Clifford's wealth was an output of shedding innocent blood and that he used the power of money to cover up all his unclean tracks. Questionably, they stared at him as he walked to the rose plant, where DCI Nyoka and Eunice had been flirting. There, he sat for a few minutes before he shifted to a palm tree, where he sat on one of six stuffed chairs.

"What did he give to Officer Nyoka?" Matthew asked warily.

"It looked like money."

"Let's leave this place right now, Stan." He stood up. "I don't trust that man at all. Where're his men? I think they hid somewhere in this park; they're plotting to kidnap us. Hurry up!" He was treading around, patting fast on his thighs. "You're slow, Stan. Let's run away!"

"Okay! Let's go!" He rose up and trotted behind him.

CHAPTER

8

ONE morning, Detective Sergeant Green Ash and his subordinates came together for a caucus in the CID conference room. He was in high spirits after receiving some information that the scratched airtime card, picked up at Mr Mpofu's house, had been used by Gilbert Mhandu, one of Clifford's men. He was also impressed by what DC Tilda had done the day before; she had checked Queen's cellphone and noted a call from Gilbert, which Queen received the very day Mr Mpofu's son was kidnapped.

"Now, we need to find out how the airtime card got into the house and also if Gilbert and Queen were both acting in cahoots. I think we should try to bring them in for interrogation."

"Mm, sir"—DC Tilda shook her head—"I think we should not take them into it so fast. I need some more time with Queen. She's likely to disclose more information to me."

Everyone nodded, except DC Bere, who opposed her: "I disagree with you, Tilda." He rose up immediately. "Our core business is to prevent crime. If we delay to stop them as soon as possible, they'll continue to commit many other crimes. You get it?"

DC Francis smirked. "Bere, you're wrong. It seems as if you're not getting on with the proceedings. You seem to be far behind. We're not here to prevent crime but to detect it. We need adequate information to lead us to the criminals who murdered Jacob Banda, Nathan Mpofu, etc. So where there's a source to provide us with the information, we don't need to disturb it. Do you understand it, Bere?"

DC Bere sat down, a bit embarrassed.

"Anyway, neither of you is wrong." Sergeant Green wrote something in his police diary. "Tilda, we're giving you more time with your newfound friend, Queen. For this whole month, don't report for duty here. We don't want people to see you frequenting these premises, or else they'll end up discovering who you're in real life. Once they know you're one of us, it means you're in hot soup and our mission will be compromised."

She beamed: "Thank you, sir."

"It's okay, Tilda.

"DC Francis and DC Bere, come with me to my office. I want to interrogate Matthew and Stanford with you. The rest, go and cover the area as usual."

They were dismissed.

Sometime later, Matthew and Stanford were back in the CID complex again. They were escorted into the interrogation room once again. This time, the temperature inside was different—it caused their jaws to shudder and their bare feet to get numbed. As usual, the room had the dim light, the stench and the eerie sound from the east.

The officer who had brought them in had just disappeared without saying anything. They could only hear the sounds of heels knocking hard onto the corridors beyond the walls and were not sure whether it was him or another person passing by.

About an hour later, DS Green and DC Francis came and unlocked the door. They took them to the office.

"Sit down!" DC Francis pushed them a little forward.

The boys sat down, their nervous faces looking at the police officers. Their hands were covered with goose pimples because of the chill in the interrogation room.

DC Bere entered the office, clutching a bunch of keys in his hand. He stared at them. "Today, you're going to perish. I've no mercy for you. With me here is a bunch of cell keys. I'm going to lock you up unless you tell us the truth." His forehead was in wrinkles.

DS Green nodded: "He's right. We'll not let you get away with this. You're being accused of stealing Bob's wallet."

Stanford's face twisted into contours of timidity. He discharged some drops of urine. He had never been into the police cells before. The little knowledge he had about them had been acquired from his uncle. He began to muse on it: *"One night, the police arrested me and put me into one of their cells. There was no light in it. It was stinking. It was like a cold room. I slept on a dirty floor. Regularly, the officers visited me and disturbed me from sleeping. In the morning, there was a little light from the sun beaming into the cell through a small window with strong burglar bars. The window was about three metres above the floor. I was dumbfounded to find out that I'd spent the whole night near a toilet chamber. On the walls, there were many engraved writings, some of which were vulgar words, and others, just funny names.*

"After two days, they—"

"Hey!" DC Francis shouted, his point shoe poking Stan into his ribs. "What're you musing on? Stand up! We don't have time to waste. The cells are empty; they need people like you."

Stanford looked at Matthew, who was already on his feet. Everything seemed to be well with him. "Let me go to the toilet first." He writhed. "I've—"

"Don't worry, Stanford." Detective Francis smirked. "There's a toilet for you in the cell."

"Let me tell you the truth, sir." He looked at Matthew, who quickly leered at him.

DC Bere frowned. "What's it? Don't waste our time here."

"If you ask Jonathan's mother, she'll tell you the truth that Bob did not lose his wallet at the party."

"Shut up! Nonsense!" DC Bere pulled him up. "Move to the cells!"

"Wait a moment." DS Green caressed his chin. "Allow them to sit down."

They sat down again.

"Who's Jonathan's mother?" Sergeant Green asked.

"It's Sherry," said Stanford, "Bob's sister. She was at the party, too."

"True, sir," Matthew said. "Her own sister will tell you the truth if she's not biased.

"I just have a question concerning the way you're handling us here. It seems as if we've committed a drastic crime. What's so special about Bob's wallet? Is it because his father was once a police boss here? Maybe that's why you're doing it like this." He burst into a suppressed cry and quickly rubbed off his tears.

DC Bere mocked him: "You think your tears can make us believe you're clean, right?"

DS Green said, "Very soon, you'll understand the whole story if you really don't know anything about it." He opened one of the desk drawers, took out the tape recorder and set it on the desk. "Allow them to sit near the desk."

The boys sat on the chairs by the desk.

The recording started.

"Good morning, boys. I'm Detective Sergeant Green Ash of the CID Homicide Section at Magamba Central Police.

"What're your names and addresses?"

One by one, they supplied their names and addresses in full.

"When we interviewed you concerning Bob's wallet, you suggested that we should question Jonathan's mother, didn't you?" The sergeant stroked his stubby beard.

"Yes, we did."

"Who's Jonathan's mother?"

"Sherry Banda, Bob's sister."

"Don't lie to us, Matthew. All of us here know Sherry Banda; she's not married, and she does not have a baby."

"It's not a lie!" Stanford blurted out: "She had a baby boy, an albino. The baby's father is unknown."

Matthew leered at him and tried to alert him through gesture that he was going out of hand and letting the cat out of the bag, but he did not notice it. Having failed to stop him, he just drooped his head.

"You say she *had* a baby; where's the baby now?"

"He died."

"Oh shame." DS Green shook his head sympathetically, inclining it to the left. "I'm very sorry about that. I'm really sorry. When did that happen?"

"Two or three weeks ago."

"Anyway, that's not the story, Stanford. Our story is about Bob's wallet. We have no business with her albino baby and so on. What we want from her is to confirm whether or not the wallet was lost at the party. Period."

Matthew sighed and raised his head.

"Now I'm going to release you, but I might need you here again after contacting Jonathan's mother possibly tomorrow."

The boys hit the road. The detectives quickly booked out to search for Sherry. When they reached her home, they found her available with her brother, Bob. Their mother, Eunice, had visited her brother in a town located about 100 kilometres away from the city of Magamba. That was what she had told her children.

The detectives took Sherry away on the pretext that they wanted her to identify some men whom they had arrested if they were the ones who kidnapped her. Bob was left with so many unanswered questions as he peered through the window, watching his sister being ushered into a white twin-cab car with no number plates. He thought of making a phone call to his mother but suddenly shook his head. The car left the place.

At the CID station, Sherry sat by the desk in DS Green's office. Near her sat a female detective whom she had never seen before. She was a stout lady with a cruel look. Her eyes were big. She never smiled at all. DS Green was on his usual chair behind the desk. DC Francis and DC Bere were by the office door. The tape recorder was on the desk.

"Jonathan's mother," DS Green called.

Sherry's heart skipped.

"I know you're shocked because I've called you in a way you never expected," he scorned. "Don't worry about that, my dear sister. It's a minor issue.

"Hmm, let me say we're not very clever detectives, though, but we've detected that you conceived an albino baby boy, who died some weeks ago. Where did you bury him?"

She remained silent and bent her head down.

The female detective blew her fuse and slapped her with the back of her hand.

The other detectives laughed: "It's just the beginning; the end will come! Wait and see!"

"Let me tell you the truth," she said, turning to her. "He was killed in the Eden Forest by the kidnappers."

"In the Eden Forest?" Sergeant Green asked, scratching his head.

She nodded quickly: "Yes, sir."

"Umm, how did that happen? Relax and tell us the truth. Don't be afraid."

"When they kidnapped me, I was with Jonathan, my son. They throttled him to death. After that, they wanted to kill me, but I fled away."

The member in charge shrugged and took the photos of the baby from one of the desk drawers. He showed them to her once again. "Last time, when we met here, I showed you these photos, didn't I?" He placed them onto the desk.

"Yes, you did."

"Whose baby is this?"

"It's mine. This is Jonathan," she sobbed.

"Your baby?"

"Yes."

"Last time, when we asked you, you said you didn't see this. You said you never had a baby. Why did you lie to us?"

"I'm sorry."

"How did your baby get into the green bag?"

"I... I... I don't know." She looked down.

"Why do you hesitate to talk? Why do you look down?"

DC Francis chipped in: "Such people are great liars."

The other detectives agreed with him.

"Do you know Nathan Mpofu?" DS Green asked.

"No."

"What about the Mpofu family that lives at Golden?"

"I don't know them."

It was stunning. How could the baby belong to two different mothers?

Sergeant Green stood up. "My sister, don't take us for fools! This baby belongs to the Mpofu family. We saw his birth records at Magamba General Hospital. Where are the birth records for your baby?"

She lowered her voice: "No records."

"Who's the father of the baby?"

She kept quiet.

DC Gava, the female detective, became angry again and slapped her. "Hey! Don't waste our time! Tell us the truth about where you dumped your real baby, not this one in the photos, who belonged to the Mpofu family! Otherwise you're one of the criminals who kidnapped their son! Yes, you killed him and dumped him in the Eden Forest."

"That's true," DC Francis said accusingly. "You're one of the gangsters who dumped Mr Mpofu's son in the Eden Forest. After committing the crime, you got lost in the jungle as you're trying to escape from your evil deeds.

"It's a lie that you're kidnapped. I think you're now going mad. At the end of the day, chickens come home to roost. How can Mrs Mpofu's baby be yours?"

"Let's lock her up," DS Green said. "She'll tell the truth in a court of law.

"Bere, collect the cell keys. She must be locked up right now."

"I've got them with me already, Serge." He patted on his pocket, and the keys clanked.

They all stood up and manhandled her to the interrogation room. When DC Bere opened the door, DC Gava pushed her in. The door was closed before she turned back. With her bare feet, she stood still on a sticky floor polish. She had never been there before.

"Get me out!" she cried.

"Stay there!" DC Gava shouted uncaringly. "That's your new home! Be generous to share it with the ghosts and the vampires!"

"No!" She staggered to the door. "Let me tell you the truth!"

"Don't take us for granted! Right?" DC Bere opened the door.

DC Gava pulled her out and dragged her along the corridor to the office. She pushed her onto the chair. "We're giving you one last chance!"

"Thank you." She was shivering. "You can ask Bob, my brother. He's the one, together with his friends, who accompanied me to the jungle to dump Jonathan's body after he had died of cholera.

"I didn't kill Mr Mpofu's son. Ask my brother or his friends, Matthew and Stanford."

"It seems as if you're now mentally challenged," DS Green said seriously. "It's better we ask Bob."

They called Bob through the phone and asked him to come for his sister. They said that they were afraid of letting her go home alone.

CHAPTER

9

AT around 4 p.m., Bob knocked on the door of DS Green's office and was called in. Suddenly, his face slouched when he saw the way his sister looked. She had a face stained with dry tears. Standing near her was a strange lady whom he had never seen before. She was not among the detectives who had come for his sister.

He greeted them all, but no one answered him. He drooped his head. Without expectation, DC Francis and DC Bere grabbed him and dragged him out of the office. All the way to the interrogation room, they did not talk to him. They pushed him in, locked the door and left. Bob screamed and screamed, but no one attended him.

Some minutes later, the male detectives left DC Gava with Sherry in the office and went to the interrogation room, where they talked to Bob from the outside.

"Bob Banda!" DS Green shouted. "Do you know why you're in there?"

"No! This is unlawful detention! I'll call my lawyer!"

"Lawyer?" They laughed. "You'll obviously do that! In case they may need to know your charge! It's murder! You're being accused of killing Sherry's baby..."

Bob's heart skipped.

"...and dumping him in the Eden Forest! She's disclosed everything to us!

"Tell us! What the hell did you do that for?"

"She's lying! Let me tell you the truth!" His voice was trembling. "I didn't kill her baby! The baby had already died of cholera when I assisted her to dump the body in the Eden Forest! I did everything under my mother's instruction!"

"Stop playing tricks with us, Bob!" DS Green laughed. "Have you taken some drugs?"

"No! You can ask my mom; she knows how it happened! She's the one who instructed us to do that! I swear!"

"Why didn't you bury him at the graveyard?" DC Francis asked.

"My mother can tell you why she made that decision!"

"Where's she?" DS Green asked.

"She visited her brother in Gutajena town."

"We'll come back to you. We want to confirm something. Stay put." He gestured at his sub-ordinates, and they smiled as they proudly walked back to the office.

They organised a plan to interview Eunice without DCI Nyoka's knowledge.

"Guys," DS Green said, enlightened, "I suspect that Jacob Banda was treated the same way Jonathan was treated."

"True, Boss."

Some minutes later, the three went back to the interrogation room and pretended as if Sherry had told them more information about the Banda family.

"Bob, we're back with more information!" DS Green shouted. "Are you there?"

"Yes!"

"Well!" He cleared his throat. "We got some more information from your sister! I understand very much that you dropped your own wallet in the Eden Forest when you were in it! What were you doing in that jungle, my good friend?"

"I... I... I'd accompanied Sherry!"

"While you're in the jungle, did you see your dead father?"

He did not answer.

"Tell us, dude! Did you kill your own father?"

He remained silent.

"Don't waste our time, boy!" DC Bere banged the door. "Are you dumb? You need some beating first before you talk, right?"

"I didn't kill him! He died of cholera!"

"Young man!" Sergeant Green banged the door. "Don't fool us! We know everything! Your father died of food poison, not cholera! A shameless liar!"

"I'm not lying, sir!"

They released him to their office and showed him the photos of the albino baby.

"This is Jonathan." Bob shed tears.

"This is incredible." DS Green shook his head and looked at his colleagues. "How about carrying the photos to the Mpofu family?"

"Good idea."

They collected the photos and drove to Golden. The time was 7 p.m.

The Mpofu family welcomed them. Without wasting time, the detectives told them the reason for the visit. The family was shown all the pictures, and they declined ownership of the baby in them. The only thing they recognised was the green faux leather bag in which their dead son was, whilst he was in the mortuary.

The detectives left the family and drove straight to the police station, where they requested for two uniformed police officers. From there, they proceeded to Mr Banda's homestead. There, they used Sherry to lie to her mother through the phone that Bob was ill.

At Bernard Hotel, Eunice received a disturbing phone call from her daughter. It came whilst she was flirting with DCI Nyoka.

"Who's he?"

"It's not *he*. It's Sherry," she replied wearily. "She says Bob is ill. What can I do now?"

"Is that true?"

"I believe so. Sherry has never told me lies."

"Umm. Let me come with you."

"No, I can't go with you. I'm afraid. They think I travelled to Gutajena town to see my brother. What'll they say if they see us together? Let me go alone. I don't want them to suspect anything between us. I'll be back very soon. If I find his condition too critical, I'll call you through the phone."

"Okay, let me call a taxi for you," he said, reaching for his cellphone.

She smiled, "Thanks, dear," and kissed him twice on his forehead.

The taxi arrived and picked her up. On her way, she called Sherry and told her that she would be home in 40 minutes. She lied that she had already left the Gutajena town and was already on her way when she received the first call. Upon hearing that, the detectives got ready for her.

About 30 minutes later, she opened the gate and rushed towards the house. Out of the blue, she saw two people, a male and a female, emerging from an open garage.

"We're police detectives from Magamba CID." DC Gava showed her a police ID card, although its writings were invisible. "You're under arrest..."

Eunice sighed. "Allow me to see my son first; he's very sick."

"Don't worry," DC Bere said. "Bob isn't sick at all. He's very fine. Look at that side." He switched on his torch.

She looked and saw Bob in handcuffs. He was standing between two uniformed police officers. There was a car behind them.

DC Bere added: "Sherry is in that car."

Her cellphone dropped. "Let me call Officer Nyoka, your boss." She bent down to pick it up.

"Stop that! You'll do it later, Madam." DC Gava pushed her away. "Bere, pick it up for her. Move to the car!"

They drove back to the station and took her to the member in charge's office for questioning. Bob and Sherry were taken to another office.

"Woman, we're here for two very serious cases," DC Gava said, glaring at her. "We're not going to handle you with kid gloves.

"We're specifically talking about the death of your husband and that of Jonathan, your grandson. Your children have already told us about your contributions to their deaths. Questioning you does not mean we know nothing; we're just doing it for formality.

"Come on. Tell us everything. How did you do it? Start with your late husband."

"My husband died of cholera."

"Cholera?" DS Green glanced at her. "For how long had he been ill?"

"For a week."

"During that period, did he go out to meet his friends or just ordinary people?"

"No, he didn't."

"This means he stayed indoors until he died, right?"

"Yes."

"After he died, what did you do next?"

"I sent Bob to dump him in the Eden Forest because I had no money for burial services."

"Umm, what was his last meal before he died?"

"Rice and chicken."

"Cholera"—he scorned—"How did you know it was it? Are you a medical practitioner?"

She said nothing.

"Didn't Officer Nyoka tell you that your husband was poisoned? Someone gave him poisoned food."

No answer.

"Take her to the interrogation room, and bring her back when she decides to tell us the truth. If she dies in there, don't worry about it. He who kills with a sword dies with a sword."

DC Gava swooped her like an eagle and pulled her out of the office. She dragged her along the corridor, hitting and kicking her. DC Bere and DC Francis were following behind them, laughing.

"Please, stop! Let me confess before I die." She was sobbing. "I want to do it in the presence of my children. Bring them for me, please."

"Woman, don't waste my time!" She frowned. "Let's go back to the office. If you don't confess, I'll bury you alive." She dragged her back to the office and forced her down onto the floor.

Bob and Sherry were brought in, and their eyes were filled with tears when they saw their mother. The detectives told them that she wanted to confess before them, so they paid attention.

Eunice looked up at her children, at Officer Green and then down.

"Get up, Mrs Banda. Sit on this comfortable chair."

She got up and sat on the chair facing Sergeant Green.

"I want you to give us full information. You can start now." He turned on the tape recorder.

"Forgive—"

"Start with your name."

"I'm Eunice Banda," she sobbed. "Forgive me, my children. I fell in love with Officer Nyoka before my husband died. As time went on, Officer Nyoka craved Sherry, my daughter, and later raped her.

"She became pregnant and gave birth to an albino baby boy, whom I named Jonathan. I kept the whole incident as a secret. My husband, Jacob Banda, did not know that his daughter had been raped by his own friend.

"When Jonathan was one year old, Officer Nyoka persuaded me to kill him and also to kill my husband so that he could marry me. Since his love had driven me crazy, I accepted his plot. He gave me some poison, which I used to kill Jacob and Jonathan. I first killed Jacob and then Jonathan.

"I lied to Bob that his father had died of cholera and persuaded him to dump his dead body in the Eden Forest. I did the same to Jonathan. Forgive me. I deserve to die."

"Is that all?" asked the member in charge.

"Yes," she said, streams of tears flowing down her face.

DS Green shook his head and switched off the tape recorder. There was a moment of silence.

"Mom, I hate you!"

"I'm sorry, Bob."

"That's useless! You killed my daddy! You're a witch! I hate you! I believed you when you talked about cholera, yet you knew your evil plans! Go to hell with your wizard, Nyoka!

"You deceived me! You persuaded me to dump my own father! God will punish you!"

"Woman"—DS Green folded his hands onto the desk—"I've found no suitable words to describe you. I just wonder how many marriages you were looking for in your life.

"Look, you're now a widow, and your children are now orphans.

"My fellow detectives, do you now see the reason Detective Chief Inspector Nyoka was preventing us from touching this family? It's because he didn't want all this mess to be revealed."

"Yes."

"Mrs Banda, do you know where he is?"

"I left him at Bernard Hotel this evening." She drooped her head.

"Okay." He reached for a telephone on the desk. "Let me contact Detective Superintendent Edwards; he'll help us arrest him."

Supt Edwards received the phone call and proceeded to his subordinate's office. When he arrived, they saluted him and gave him a seat. He sat down, gaping at Eunice and her children. Immediately, DS Green told him on the whole story.

"Grr!" He hit the top of the desk. "Where's this bloody Nyoka? I need him!"

Eunice told him.

Supt Edwards and DS Green made a strategy to arrest him. They took Eunice to her home and let her use her cellphone to call him; meanwhile, they mounted an ambush.

"Honey, Bob is very sick. I need your help."

"What happened to him?" Slowly, he stroked the bridge of his nose.

"I don't know."

"It's okay; I'll be there soon. Is the main gate open?"

"It's closed, but let me keep it open for you."

"Thanks."

"Bye." She kissed him through the phone.

The police officers waited for him, armed with pistols.

"Be very vigilant, my friends," Supt Edwards warned his team. "You all know the man we're making this ambush for. He's a trained detective who always carries his pistol."

"Thank you, sir," Sergeant said.

At that moment, DC Bere and DC Gava were at the station, guarding Bob and Sherry.

DCI Nyoka passed through the city centre of Magamba, negligently driving against red robots and overtaking other vehicles where it was prohibited to do so. Traffic police cars tried to pursue him, but they did it in vain. When he reached Eunice's home, he got out of the car and hurried towards the house.

"Hands up!" A familiar voice shot from the dark.

He looked around and saw three detectives and five uniformed police officers surrounding him.

"I said hands up!" Supt Edwards said again. "Don't move! You're under arrest!"

He slowly lifted up his hands, asking rudely, "I'm under arrest for what?"

"For rape and murder," he said, advancing to him.

"This is an unlawful arrest; I'll sue you, motherfucker!" he said; meanwhile, DS Green handcuffed him.

"You've the right to remain silent!" Supt Edwards warned him. "Anything you say will be used against you in the court of law!"

"That's nonsense to me! You're lucky that I left my gun!

"You're wasting your time; I'm a well-connected person. I'll get away with this!"

They dragged him to a police car, where he was shocked to see Eunice in handcuffs.

The two were detained at the police station. Bob and Sherry were released on summons. A memorandum of arrest in respect of Detective Chief Inspector Nyoka was written fast and dispatched to the superiors.

Two days later, they were released from the police custody to the courts of law, where DCI Nyoka was sentenced to 70 years in prison and Eunice, to 50 years. The court suspended 40 years from Eunice's jail term on condition that she was the only parent left for her family.

CHAPTER
10

THE following day, Sister Faith embraced Sherry, in her office. She was rubbing tears off her bitter face.

"Look at Thandiwe." She patted her on her back. "She stayed with the Mpofu family. Now, she's back with us..." The principal took Sherry's orphanage file from the desk and put it aside.

Sherry sobbed: "My story is different from Thandiwe's. I stayed with the Banda family, not knowing I was just an adopted child in the family. I—"

"I'm sorry, Sherry."

She began to think about the lady who once picked her up when she was with Daniel in the Eden Forest. The lady said that her name was Gertrude Jena, and she showed that she knew her and Jacob Banda very well. Sherry also remembered Daniel saying they looked like sisters.

"Sister Faith, life doesn't make sense for me. I see no reason to survive in this world."

"Don't say that again, my love."

"Why should I remain silent? God created me to suffer on this damned earth. He allowed the death of my mother. Today, I'm rubbish. I wasted my time with a wrong family that spoiled my whole life. I don't even know my father. Look, Sister, for about 16 years, I've been calling wrong people my parents. Is this good?"

"Sorry, Sherry. Calm down. I understand your situation. You're not alone; everyone here is an orphan. I also grew up as an orphan, but here I'm with my happy family. This isn't the end of the world. God loves you that's why He spared you. Only the devil is a liar; he came to steal and destroy, but God is there to save.

"We have many prominent men and ladies who're rich today, but they grew up as orphans without parental support. That's how many of us grow up. Almost 70% of the children grow up without their parents, especially in these days when there are many diseases and unspeakable vehicle accidents..." Sister Faith talked and talked until Sherry calmed down.

The news spread everywhere that Sherry was not the real child of Jacob Banda and Eunice Banda. The detectives heard it and felt sorry for her.

*

Two days later, the detectives met in the office of the member in charge and discussed the case of the albino baby.

"We need to visit Magamba Mortuary for some investigations," DS Green said. "Someone killed Nathan to replace the body of Jonathan."

"That's it."

They left the office. When they arrived at the mortuary, they were allowed to check the mortuary registers, two of which had anomalies—a certain police officer had booked out the keys in the mortuary keys register but had not written anything in the dead body register.

"This is an eye opener." DS Green showed his colleagues the registers. "When a person books out the keys for the mortuary, they also use a dead body register to book in or out the dead body. But this one here is different. This person booked out the keys but did not use the dead body register. You see?"

They nodded.

"And this is a fake force number," DC Francis said. "This is a bogus police officer."

"You're right," the others agreed.

They went and checked a security occurrence book at the main gate. Only one white twin-cab car without number plates was recorded during the night in question. The security officers revealed that the car was being driven by Officer Nyoka and it was the one that DS Green and his colleagues had come driving on that day.

Now, the detectives waited to hear more information from Sister Joyce, a Magamba General Hospital worker whose office was responsible for keeping all the keys of the hospital premises. She was the one on duty when the bogus officer booked out the keys.

*

The night that followed, Tilda and Queen were at Bernard Bar. Bob got in and walked up to the buffet, where he purchased an expensive beer. He sat on a stool and began to drink, watching female strippers. A tender hand touched his shoulder; he looked up and saw Queen standing near him, a dazzling smile on her lips. His first encounter with her was at Matthew's home.

Tilda tried by all means to avoid Bob from seeing her with Queen, but it was too late; he had already noticed it.

After some minutes, Queen went to Diesel and whispered something into his ear for some seconds. Diesel cast his eyes at Bob and then at Razor.

She walked back to Bob. "Diesel is like an uncle to me. I just whispered to him that I'm going out with Bob. I did so; in case, he might get worried about my whereabouts."

"It's okay. I see no problem with that. Let's go right now."

She smiled and grabbed him out of the bar. They got a taxi.

After thirty minutes, Diesel glanced at his wristwatch and winked at Razor. They both left the bar. Everything was happening within DC Tilda's sight, and she became uneasy about the situation now at hand.

Bob was already in bed, making love with Queen. He had never been treated like that before. "I saw you with Tilda; who's she to you?"

"She's just a friend of mine." She was caressing his chest. "Do you know her?"

"Yes, of course. If I didn't know her, would I call her by her name?"

She stopped caressing him. "From where do you know her?"

"She's a detective." He looked her in the eyes.

Her heart skipped. "What do you mean?"

"She's a police detective at Magamba CID Station. Got it?"

She rolled her lips into her mouth. *Okay, this is what she is. I trusted her and told her every secret. She's going to pay for it.*

"What're you thinking about? Are you not okay?" He kissed her on the right cheek. "Let's have another—"

"Don't move." Diesel pointed his pistol at Bob, with Razor following behind him.

Queen got up and joined them. They tied him to his bed and taped his mouth.

"Kill him," Queen told Diesel. "If he lives, he'll tell the police."

"Tilda must die, too. She's a cop."

"Fuck! A cop?" Diesel got angry and released a bullet into Bob's head. "Let's go find Tilda!"

"We loot the property first!" Razor said. "We have to leave with—"

"No!" Queen shook her head. "No time for that, Razor! We're *gonna* busted here!"

They rushed out and drove to Bernard Bar to eliminate Tilda, but they did not find her. She was now in one of the police cars attending the scene at Jacob Banda's home.

"We're late," DS Green said. "They've already left."

The gate and the main door of the house were wide open. Some of the police officers slipped in, cocked guns in their hands, and searched every room. The other ones were led out by DC Tilda to all the areas she expected to find the gangsters.

In one of the rooms, Bob's lifeless body lay in a pool of blood. The detectives searched the room and found a video camera covered with a book; now, it was recording the bed and half of the dead body.

They played the video at the police station. It showed that Queen, Diesel and Razor were responsible for the death of Bob Banda, so a manhunt to apprehend them was launched.

CHAPTER

11

THE detectives held a meeting in which DC Tilda shared the information that she had acquired from Queen.

"Thank you, sir, for this opportunity," she smiled. "Good morning, everyone."

"Good morning."

"I got much information about Clifford Kauri and Detective Chief Inspector Nyoka from Queen. Detective Chief—"

"No, Tilda!" DS Green put his hand up. "Don't call him Detective Chief Inspector Nyoka. He's now Mr Nyoka or Nyoka without any title."

They laughed.

"Thank you, sir. Well, allow me to continue."

Everyone paid attention.

"Nyoka is the one who plotted the kidnapping and killing of Nathan Mpofu. In the deal, he worked with Gilbert Mhandu and Queen, whom he sent to kidnap the baby. Gilbert is the one who entered the house through the back window and took him away while Queen engrossed Thandiwe, the maid, with colourful clothes, which she pretended to sell.

"They carried Nathan's body to the mortuary and replaced the one of Jonathan with it." She paused to receive some comments.

"It links perfectly well with what we got from the hospital security yesterday," said Sergeant Green. "They saw Nyoka driving in and out our twin-cab carrying a loaded body bag in the loading pan."

The others nodded: "Sure."

"So if Gilbert Mhandu, Clifford's man, is involved in this crime, it means his boss is also involved," DC Francis said accusingly.

She shook her head: "No. Clifford isn't a killer at all and has never been into killing. All his men, except this Mhandu, are not killers, and I heard that he was fired from work because of Nathan's death. This means he's no longer Clifford's man.

"Clifford is just a drug dealer. All his businesses are products of his drug dealings. It's alleged that he has a secret place in the Eden Forest where he hides all types of drugs. It's a well-built underground storeroom. I suggest you alert the CID Drug Section detectives about this."

DC Gava smirked: "For many years, this man has been supporting the police with many resources. His illicit deals started many years ago, and no one has ever arrested him up to this date. Do you think all those officers who worked before us were incompetent? And these—"

DS Green chipped in: "Where's Gilbert Mhandu?"

"His whereabouts are not known at the moment."

"Okay."

DC Bere asked, "Who was the mortuary attendant?"

"No one," she said. "They don't work during the night; that's the problem."

DS Green nodded: "Sure; that's why Nyoka and his accomplices got the chance to replace Jonathan's body. They couldn't do that in the presence of a mortuary attendant.

"What about Sister Joyce, the lady in charge of the keys? Is she involved in the mess? She was the one on duty when it happened."

"She's smart. Nyoka just took advantage of that police officers on duty are allowed to book out the mortuary keys any time they want to convey a dead body into the mortuary."

"I see." He nodded. "But still we have to record a statement from her when she's back next week. Now, she's on leave."

They agreed.

"Now I understand why Clifford's biplane makes several trips to and fro the Eden Forest. It's because of his drugs hidden in the jungle."

*

At Magamba Maximum Prison, the prisoners were on a maize field carpeted with weeds. Among them, there were Mrs Banda and Mr Nyoka. In their perspiring hands, they held blunt hoes. As they worked, fierce dogs monitored them. The dogs snarled every time the prisoners stretched out their backs. Although it was a small number of them, they moved around, untethered, and appeared as if they were many. Eunice felt her body itching from sweat but could not scratch it; Tiger was gnarling and leering at her.

Apart from the dogs, there were the prison officers guarding them, armed with guns. Even though they were to be left alone, no one could climb up the tallest electrified durawall of the prison.

Eunice gripped her hoe so tightly that her hands ached with pain. One of the female prison officers approached her. "Woman, you're wanted at our offices urgently. Let's go."

She smiled. That was her time to rest. She left the field, under escort.

"Good morning, Eunice Banda. I'm P.O. Bero," the prison officer introduced herself.

"Good morning, Madam."

"Hmm, I'm sorry to announce this. Hmm, we've received, eh, some bad news that your house was attacked by robbers. And, hmm, your son was shot dead."

"What? Bob—" She collapsed.

*

An hour later, at the CID station, the detectives were summing up their meeting agendas when Detective Sergeant Green Ash dipped his hand into one of his pockets and fished out his vibrating cellphone. With narrowed eyes, he glanced at it and noticed an incoming call from his friend who worked at Magamba Maximum Prison. The other detectives maintained some reasonable silence to allow him to answer it.

After the dialogue, he looked sorrowful and put the phone onto the table. "Eunice Banda has breathed her last. She collapsed to death soon after receiving the news about Bob."

"Oh shame!"

"This means we have to attend this scene.

"What spell has fallen upon Jacob Banda's family? The whole family is no more."

"I suspect avenging spirits," DC Gava said. "Maybe one of their ancestors shed innocent blood. At the end of the day, chickens come home to roost. The results of everything we do come to rest upon us at the end."

DC Bere shook his head: "There is nothing like the existence of avenging spirits. When people die, they die for good. You, people, have wrong beliefs."

She clicked her tongue. "You just oppose without reasoning. Avenging spirits have been there since *kare*. They're even spoken of in the Bible. Go and read from it. One day you'll believe their existence."

"Don't refer me to the Bible; I'm not a Christian," he retorted.

"Time's up," DS Green intercepted their dialogue. "Let's attend the scene."

The meeting was brought to an end, and they left the place.

*

At 10 a.m., the prisoners stopped working. They gathered under a large tree and queued for pieces of bread and some tea. In their hands, they held metal cups and metal plates.

"Time's up!" one of the prison officers shouted. "You didn't come here for food but for work! Pick up your hoes! No time to waste!"

Without choice, they picked up their hoes and walked to the field. Some of them had not finished their food.

*

The following day, Sherry mourned in Sister Faith's office after receiving the news about Eunice and Bob. Everyone at the OCCO centre sympathised with her.

"Sorry, dear." Sister Faith patted her on her back. "Life has a lot to offer. God remembers you day and night. He has got a bright future for you. This period of mourning shall come to pass. No situation is bound to stay forever. Calm down, dear."

"This is too much, Sister. Does God really love me?"

"Don't say that again. God loves you very much. He does things for a purpose. You have a bright future, my dear."

An hour later, Sherry went to join her friends playing soccer and netball on the grounds. They enjoyed the sports for three hours. She was the best netball player and was promising to be the best all over the world. Everyone admired her.

"Excuse me," she said to her fellow players, "let me respond to the call of nature."

"It's okay," the team leader said. "Anyone from the terraces to replace Sherry?"

There was nobody to substitute her, so they waited for her to come back.

"She's taking too long," one of the spectators complained.

The other ones agreed with nods. They turned their heads only to find Thandiwe sprinting from the toilets. She was screaming and shouting: "Sister Faith! Sister Faith!"

Everyone ran to her. "What happened?"

She answered no one. She was just pointing at the toilets.

Sister Faith and her workmates met her. She led them back to the toilets, where they were greatly shocked to see Sherry swinging from a fixed beam. Her neck was tied in a loop, and her tongue lay outside on her lower lip. There were poop and wee-wee under her, and her legs had tracks of them from her underwear. Tears had left lines from her open eyes. Everyone wept as they saw her in that state.

Immediately, the principal called the police.

*

One week later, Daniel Sango visited DS Green and told him everything about his nightmares.

"I get it, Daniel." He looked troubled. "This is strange. How many times has your late father appeared to you in the dreams?"

"More than three times in every week. His message is the same: 'Go to the Eden Forest and search for my treasure, which I lost 16 years ago'.

"I always wonder what type of treasure it is, the one that can last for such a very long period without depreciating. This is incredible. I tried to ignore it, but the dreams continue disturbing me. I sometimes see a red snake with black spots in the dreams. This is strange.

"Last time, not in a dream, I saw this snake in the Eden Forest. If you ask Sherry Banda, she'll tell you the same. She also saw it."

"I'm sorry, Sherry Banda died a week ago."

"Hey! Dead? What happened to her?"

"She committed suicide after receiving the news about the deaths of Eunice and Bob, her family members."

"Oh shame, what happened to them?"

"Bob was shot dead by armed robbers. Eunice died of shock when she heard about Bob's sudden death. That's how it happened."

"You see?" He shed little tears. "That's why I kindly request you to accompany me to the Eden Forest; I'm afraid of these ruthless murderers. They murdered my father in that jungle. In the same way, they can also kill me."

"Don't worry, I'll go with you. The day to come after tomorrow, I'll be on a three-day time off. That's the day we must set off on our journey to the jungle."

"Thank you, my brother; thank you."

"Serge"—DC Francis approached DS Green—"I'm through with Sister Joyce's statement. May I let her go?"

"Let me check it first." He reached for the statement.

He handed it over to him. "I overheard you talking about going to the Eden Forest. Am I allowed to join the team? I've got a six-day time off starting from tomorrow."

Daniel smiled at him.

"If you're willing, we have no problem with that, Francis." DS Green handed the statement back to him. "A good statement. Let the witness go home."

"Thank you, Serge."

The lady was dismissed.

"Serge," DC Francis asked soon after Daniel had left the police station, "is it true that Daniel's father was the biological father of Sherry? People say he killed Gertrude Jena because she had threatened to expose their affair to his wife. After killing her, he committed suicide in the Eden Forest."

"I don't know. I only know that the two were found dead in the Eden Forest. They both died within the same time, and their dead bodies were discovered lying close to each other.

"Gertrude died of food poison, whereas Walter Sango was stabbed with a knife. Maybe what you're saying is true, but I doubt it."

"Considering Jacob Banda's expertise, during his time as a detective, had the accused person been surviving after the commission of that crime, he would have been busted before we joined the police force. This is true, Serge. I see no reason for you to doubt it. Haha."

"Who knows?" DS Green smiled. "If God is willing, he'll disclose the truth to us by any means."

"As for me, I'm convinced to believe that Walter Sango was the biological father of Sherry. Just look at the coincidence Sherry and Daniel once had in the Eden Forest for the first time. It meant a lot about their relationship."

"Haha. You talk too much. Anyway, what you're saying is believed by almost everyone."

Two days later, the three drove to the Eden Forest, where they arrived late in the morning and began to search randomly for the treasure.

DC Francis stopped. "Didn't your father tell you the exact place to find the thing? This jungle is too big."

"He didn't."

"In that case, I'm going to the car; you see me there."

"Don't discourage us, Francis," DS Green complained. "Anyway, go to the car." He threw the car key to him. "Just be careful; this jungle has sacred animals, the dangerous ones."

He picked it up and returned it to him. "Take it. I'm not going."

"Afraid of the animals?" DS Green laughed.

Suddenly, it started raining. There was nowhere to hide, except in a cave of a baobab tree nearby. The cave was familiar to Daniel; he had once taken shelter in it. It was dark, so DS Green switched on his torch. The place was warm and clean. It looked as if someone was using it daily.

"Ah!" Sergeant Green looked around. "Is this... Who lives in this cave?"

"Clifford's men," DC Francis said, also turning around. "Remember what Tilda said: They have a drug storeroom in this jungle."

"I think you're correct."

Daniel just looked at them without saying anything.

They sat down.

"What's that thing I see in that hole?" The sergeant asked and stood up.

Daniel and DC Francis got up and trotted out.

"Run away!" Daniel shouted. "That's the snake I told you about!"

Contrary to the warning, he advanced to it. He checked and pulled it from the hole. It was a pouch with its camera. "Come in. It's just a camera!"

They walked in, their hearts still unsteady. They only relaxed when they found out that he was telling the truth.

"Fuck!" DS Green clicked his tongue. "It has flat batteries.

"I suppose this was left here by Clifford's men. We've to find out if it contains anything of police interest. Let's carry it away." He put it back into the pouch.

"Good idea, but from where shall we get new batteries of this old type?" DC Francis asked worriedly.

"If we can't get them," DS Green said, "we'll just remove the memory card from the camera; it has got a removable card in its pot."

"Don't worry about the batteries; I've got them at home," Daniel said. "My father left me with three cameras of this type."

"Really?" DS Green smiled at him. "So we're done with this. Let's leave this place before its owners find us here."

They left the cave and headed out of the jungle to their car.

At Daniel's home, they put the charged batteries into the camera, but it did not work.

"How about cleaning the terminals of the camera first?" Daniel said.

The detectives nodded: "Good idea."

They cleaned the terminals and then inserted the batteries.

"Wow!" DS Green exclaimed. "It's working!"

They closed up and watched an incredible video showing three people: a man, a woman and a baby girl, who were eating their food. Suddenly, the woman collapsed and writhed on the ground, foam coming out of her mouth. The man did not help her; instead, he stood up, carefully picked up her leftovers and threw them away. As he walked back to his position, he stopped immediately and stared at the camera. He advanced to it. The camera swerved and began to record the bushes and the legs of the person holding it, who was now running away. Finally, it recorded his panicking face before he pushed it into its pouch.

Daniel cried; that was his father's face.

After watching it repeatedly, DS Green took it to his superiors.

*

Three days later, Daniel visited DS Green at his workplace.

~ 126 ~

"The day before yesterday, we submitted the video to the experts to examine it. They said they need a witness statement from you confirming that the person in the video is Walter Sango, your father.

"Two of Getrude Jena's relatives submitted theirs already. As for Jacob Banda, the police submitted it on behalf of his non-existing relatives."

"No problem, Officer Green. I can write it now."

"It's okay." He took a plain paper and a pen from one of the desk drawers and handed them over to him. "Everyone confirmed that the killer is Jacob Banda. The lady is Gertrude Jena. The baby is Sherry. The cameraman is your father."

"Before I write the statement, there's something I want to tell you about."

"Go ahead."

"After you had left with the video that day, I saw my father and Gertrude in a dream. They both told me their stories.

"Gertrude said, 'My name's Gertrude Jena. I'm the mother of Sherry. I was Jacob Banda's side chick. When Sherry was about two years old, I threatened to disclose our affair to Jacob's wife. Afraid of it, he lured me to the Eden Forest and poisoned me to death.' Tears were flowing down her cheeks.

"After saying that, my father came close to me, and we shook hands. He said, 'Thank you for finding the treasure. The camera with its video is the treasure. When it was all happening in the jungle, I was recording a video, whose progress was interrupted when Jacob Banda spotted me. I ran away as fast as I could and hid the camera in a baobab cave. From the cave, I ran south, but luck escaped me; Jacob tackled me down and stabbed me to death. He then carried my corpse and dumped it a few metres away from Gertrude's.'" Daniel sobbed.

"It's okay, Dan. Calm down."

He rubbed off his tears and continued: "After my father, Gertrude added that Jacob then carried Sherry to the OCCO centre. From there, he went home and convinced her wife to adopt a baby girl. And they adopted Sherry."

"This means Eunice was not aware that Sherry was her husband's real daughter, right?"

"Who's Eunice?"

"Jacob's wife."

"Oh, yes, she wasn't aware of that."

The detective sighed. "Now I understand what Gava said about the avenging spirits. Bere argued with her, but she was right. Chickens come home to roost. The results of our deeds eventually come to rest upon us. Jacob's family has perished because of his evil works. He shed innocent blood. Like drops of heavy rain falling onto the ground, the blood of the innocent falls heavily onto its enemies for revenge.

"I feel sorry for Sherry; she died with wrong information that the man in question was not his biological father. Not forgetting Eunice and Bob. They all died without this latest information. Life isn't fair."

"Should I include this dream in my statement?"

"No." He shook his head. "This will not work as evidence. But you can record it somewhere just to keep it as part of your history records."

"Thank you."

DC Tilda knocked on the door and entered: "Sir, I got a phone call from Detective Assistant Inspector Masiye of the CID Border Control Unity. He said that Queen, Gilbert, Diesel and Razor have been arrested at Wide Forest Border."

"Wow! That's great!" He jumped up from his chair. "We don't have time to waste; let's go for them now!"

A group of ten armed detectives left the station for Queen, Gilbert, Diesel and Razor. The following day, they escorted them back to Magamba Central Police Station.

After two days, they appeared before Judge Patson Mazira, facing murder charges. Nyoka was also among them for a fresh count of murder. He was being accused of killing Nathan Mpofu, and the judge sentenced him to death. Queen, Diesel, Razor and Gilbert were sentenced to life in prison.

*

"Ladies and gentlemen, I'm happy," Detective Inspector Green Ash said cheerfully. "I welcome you all to this party. You're celebrating with me for my promotion. I was promoted a week ago from the rank of a sergeant to the rank of an inspector. It's not by my own power or wisdom, but it's by the grace of God. Therefore, I praise and thank Him.

"It's not easy to work under pressure, but it needs patience and persistence. All my work-mates know the challenges I faced in trying to bring the criminals to the face of the law. It wasn't easy. Not only did the challenges affect me, but they also affected my subordinates. Why so? It's because we worked together in unity as a team.

"I thank Officer Tilda for her braveness; she managed to stay with the criminals for some time, studying their ways. It's not an easy as-signment to carry. She deserves a prize of honour, and I'll sort it for her.

"I also acknowledge Officer Francis, Officer Gava, Officer Bere and many others for their unspeakable support. You're excellent, my team. I'm what I am because of you.

"Finally, I thank Daniel Sango. He's been committed to assisting the police in many ways until now.

"Thank you very much, everybody."

The whole community was in high spirits because of its committed police officers. Eve-ryone ate and drank.

One of the guests stood up and passed a comment: "I feel comfortable in a community with police officers like Officer Green and his team." He paused and sipped his drink. "Polic-ing is really from the heart. It's a calling. Keep it up, our beloved officer. I'm happy for you. Speaking on behalf of those who support me, we promise to work hand in hand with you. Thank you so much."

Everyone clapped their hands, and there were shouts of joy.

*

At Magamba Maximum Prison, Queen sat in her prison cell. Since the day she came in, she had not been sleeping well. Her blankets were stinking, and some lice were masticating her every night. The walls of the room were caked with green stuff, which appeared as thin layers of faeces, and were engraved with obscene writings. She wondered if the other rooms were like that. In one of the four corners, there was a toilet chamber, which was flashed once a day.

"Do these prison officers care about me? They don't clean the walls for me. They don't even flash the toilet in time, umm. Anyway, I think I deserve more than this because of what I did; I contributed in the killings of two innocent souls. For sure, I deserve to die, too." She cried and moved around, shaking her head and disheveling her hair. She tried to tear her prison clothes. "Why didn't you, motherfuckers, sentence me to death?" She took down her trousers. "At the end of the day, chickens come home to roost! Yes! See them! They're here! I see Bob and Nathan! Drive them away, please!

"Hey! Look over there! Some drops of blood are falling down like drops of rain! What's going on? Is the roof damaged? Where's my bed? My toilet chamber? I can't see them! O! Where's my body? Where's me? I can't see myself! I can't feel my body! Where's it? Am I dead? What the hell is going on here? See a pool of blood on the floor! Whose blood is this?"

In the morning, the prison officers found her dead in a pool of blood on the floor. She had bled the most from her mouth and her nose. Her forehead and her knuckles had sustained severe injuries. On the walls, there were smears and writings in blood: *Chickens Come Home to Roost.*

—The End—

www.ingramcontent.com/pod-product-compliance
Lightning Source LLC
Chambersburg PA
CBHW071316130626
46556CB00004B/1626